DEAN'S LIST

A STANDALONE FROM THE GONE TRILOGY

Stacy Claflin

http://www.stacyclaflin.com

To receive book updates from the author, sign up here.
http://bit.ly/1ONrfMw

Discovery

LYDIA HARRIS FOCUSED on her phone conversation, not paying attention to her actions as she got ready for a night out with the girls. She headed into the closet to find the perfect top to go with her adorable new shorts. She forgot she carried her glass perfume bottle, and her fingers slid as her left flip-flop caught on the corner of the molding of the large walk-in closet.

"Are we meeting for drinks first? I want—"

The perfume bottle slid from her hand, heading straight for Dean's treasured safe. It was the one where they kept the really important things, like money and jewelry.

Lydia watched in horror, the blood draining from her face, as the little glass container appeared to move in slow motion.

"Are you there, Lyds?" asked Bri.

Lydia let the phone fall onto the carpet as she reached for the perfume bottle. Her middle finger grazed it, pushing it closer toward the safe.

It hit, and broke instantly, sending glass in all directions. The strong smell surrounded her as she watched the liquid run down the front and sides of the safe, moving its way inside.

Lydia picked the phone back up. "I've got to go, Bri. Can you tell everyone I'm going to be a little late? Now I have a mess to clean up."

"Oh." Bri's pout could be heard through the phone. "Can't you leave the mess for the housekeeper?"

"No. Dean's due back tonight, and housekeeping won't be here until Tuesday. I have to take care of this now."

"How late?" Bri asked.

"Hopefully not long, but if you guys have to start without me, then go ahead."

"I'm sure we can wait, sweetie. See you soon."

"Bye," Lydia said, ending the call. She stared at the mess, not knowing where to start.

Dean was almost never home, but when he was, he was extremely particular about keeping things clean. And by clean, he meant perfect. If she left behind even a shard of glass or drop of sticky perfume, he would know, and would let her hear about it, too.

Lydia picked up the nozzle from the perfume and the larger pieces of glass, and walked back to the bathroom. Wrapping them in a paper towel and put them in the garbage, she opened the windows in the bathroom and the bedroom, and then grabbed the rest of the paper towels.

Staring at the mess in the closet, she again tried to decide the best way to get rid of all traces of her mistake. Lydia pulled off a few paper towels and used them to pick up the small pieces of glass. She was relieved to see how many stuck. When she had most of them picked up, she went back into the bathroom and threw the paper towels away.

Lydia brought the garbage back into the closet with her so she could throw each remaining shard of glass into the bin. She got on her knees and picked up the tiny shards stuck to the carpet fibers with her long, manicured nails. When she was sure she had gotten every last piece, she spun the dial and opened the safe door. Perfume ran down the inside of the door.

At least it hadn't gotten on anything inside. She wiped everything with the paper towels, but it wasn't enough. Lydia went back into the bathroom for a spray bottle of cleaner. After she was sure that every trace of the perfume and its bottle were gone, she gave it a once-over and then noticed something underneath the safe. It looked like her perfume may have pooled up there.

Lydia groaned, not wanting to move the heavy thing. She slid her finger along the bottom, and sure enough, underneath the safe it was wet. There was no other choice.

She moved the garbage bin and the paper towels out into the bedroom, and then stared at the safe. It was good sized, but not enormous. It wouldn't be impossible to move, but it would take some work. She wrapped her arms around the back of it and pulled, grunting. It moved about an inch. She repeated the process until the safe was out of the way—and she was covered in sweat.

Sure enough, there was a spot where the perfume pooled underneath the safe. She was going to have to get the liquid and the smell out of the carpet. Lydia went back into the bedroom to grab the paper towels and the spray bottle again.

Several minutes into the cleaning process, her phone rang. Lydia stared at the mess in the closet, shaking her head. She grabbed her phone, knowing that it was Bri. She was right. "Bri, I'm sorry, but I won't be able to make it today."

"Oh, Lyds. Don't bail on us."

"Sorry, but you know how Dean gets about his stuff. He's going to be back tonight, and I made a huge mess."

"Well, if you can make it come down, okay?"

"I'll try. Tell the girls hi for me."

"Will do. See you later, sweetie."

"Bye, Bri." Lydia threw her phone on the bed and then grabbed a flashlight. She went into the closet and shone the light over the carpet to make sure she hadn't missed any glass.

She was about to turn the flashlight off when something on the carpet caught her eye. Lydia wouldn't have noticed it without the brighter light. Part of the carpet was a slightly different color than the rest. She knelt down and shone the light closer. A patch of the carpet was just a shade lighter.

They had never replaced any of the carpet. She would have remembered, because Dean hated stuff like that. If something was wrong, he would have simply had all of it replaced. He would much rather throw money at something than accept a substandard version.

That was how he treated Lydia as well.

She leaned over and pulled on the lighter part, and the entire piece came off. Lydia stared at it and set it down, eyes widening. It looked like there was a groove in the wood flooring.

Lydia slid her finger into the channel and pulled. The wood came up, exposing a box underneath. Her heart pounded in her chest. She had to remove two more pieces of wood to get the box out.

It was made out of a material similar to the safe, but didn't appear to be as strong. She held her breath as she looked over the box.

Did she dare open it? She'd gone this far, she couldn't just put it back without seeing what was inside. She crossed her legs and set it on her lap.

Lydia's breath caught as she reached for the latch. What was she going to find? Was it something that had belonged to the previous homeowner? Or something of Dean's?

If so, it could be paperwork laying out some kind of shady deal he'd made with a client. It wouldn't surprise her, given how secretive he always was about his work.

Whatever it was, it had to be good for Dean to go to so much trouble to hide it. He was home only about three days a month, so she was impressed that he had managed all of this without her knowing.

She pulled on the latch, and the top came off with a creak. The box was full of newspaper clippings. Lydia dug around, looking for whatever was hiding beneath the papers.

Nothing.

Lydia unfolded the first paper and looked at the headline. It was a story about a housewife in Detroit who had been murdered. Chills ran down her back, despite the warm summer weather.

She set the paper down and unfolded the next one. A waitress from Boston slain.

Lydia looked at the next one. A hotel manager from San Diego killed under suspicious circumstances.

A librarian from Houston murdered in cold blood.

Everything around Lydia disappeared as she read the headlines from each of the papers. Her ears rang, drowning out other sounds. Dread washed over her as she realized that Dean had been to every one of the cities when he traveled for work. Would his work schedule match the dates on the papers?

Her stomach lurched.

Why would he keep those clippings? Surely he'd have a good reason to save and then hide them.

She went into the bedroom to look at the time. It was later than she thought, and Dean was due back in a little over an hour. That wasn't much time to get everything back in order.

Lydia grabbed a notebook and took it back to the closet. She wrote down the dates and cities of each murder on one of the pages.

Then she snapped a picture of each clipping on her phone. She had some digging to do, but it would have to wait until after Dean left again.

She folded the clippings with great care. If anything was even slightly off, Dean would notice right away. She put each paper in exactly as she had found it, and then closed the lid. She slipped the box into the floor and then put the pieces of wood back. Getting the carpet back as it had been was trickier, but she managed.

Lydia's nerves were on fire as she pushed the safe back into place.

Then she put some baking soda down on the carpet and vacuumed, hoping that would bring out the scent. It did seem to help—hopefully enough. Dean could be hyper-aware of tiny details.

She double-checked everything to make sure the perfume was fully cleaned up and that not a piece of glass remained. Once she was certain everything looked untouched, she tied up the garbage bag and took it to the bin outside.

A bead of sweat ran down her forehead. Lydia wiped it away, and went back upstairs to her room. She folded the paper she had written the dates and cities on and slid it into one of her steamy romance novels, where he would never look for it. Then she changed the password to her phone. She couldn't risk Dean accidentally finding the pictures she'd taken of the clippings.

She slid her phone into her shorts pocket and went back up to the bedroom so she could take a shower. The mixture of the perfume and sweat offended her nose, and Dean would definitely complain when he got home. Not that he would want to touch her, and for the first time, Lydia was grateful for that.

She went into the closet to grab some clean clothes. The smell of the perfume lingered, but wasn't nearly as bad as it had been. If she could keep Dean away from the bedroom for a little while, he would never know anything had been spilled—or moved.

Lydia shook as she grabbed a sleeveless top from the hanger. She wanted to be wrong, to believe that the clippings meant something else, but how could they? Why else would he go to all that trouble to hide them?

Dean obviously wanted to save them, and clearly not digitally since that would probably leave a trail.

Lydia put her new clothes on the bathroom counter and then went into one of the guest rooms and grabbed a fan. She plugged it in by the window next to her side of the bed and turned it on, facing the window. The fragrant air needed to be pushed outside. She lit a candle, too.

Lydia finished showering and getting ready just before she expected Dean to arrive. Her pulse quickened at the thought of talking to him. Usually, he preferred to avoid her as much as possible. He averaged three nights with her every thirty days, and she used the term 'with her' generously. He'd be in the house, but they wouldn't be together.

Often that bothered her. This time she dreaded his return. And prayed they wouldn't spend any time with each other.

His job required him to travel, but Lydia had always been certain that it didn't demand that much. He had to offer it up. She always assumed it was because he was having affairs. Never in a million years would she have guessed it was anything like this.

Lydia fluffed her hair, put the fan back in the guest room, and went downstairs. Everything was still quiet, which meant he wasn't home yet. Dean stomped around like the king of a castle, making sure Lydia knew it was his domain, and that he could do what he wanted.

She paced back and forth between the living room and the kitchen.

Maybe just the fact that she was home was enough to alert him that something was wrong. It might be better if she joined her friends, even though she was already really late.

She heard the sounds of the garage door opening. Dean's arrival made the decision for her.

Dinner

LYDIA HEARD HIS engine cut in the garage. She jumped, her pulse pounding in her ears.

Dean would know she found his papers. Then he would kill her, too.

She took a deep breath. There was no reason for him to suspect she had found his things.

Lydia ran to the kitchen and pulled out some food. She would have to distract herself with cooking to keep from acting like something was wrong.

It had been a while since she'd made her famous lasagna for him. Lydia had planned on making some for dinner with the girls the next night—it was her night to take care of the meal—so she already had everything in the fridge. The homemade noodles and sauce would be enough to help put Dean in a good mood.

She pulled out all the ingredients for that and got to work. Just as she got the meat into the frying pan, she looked up to see Dean walking in.

Lydia forced a smile and said, "Hi."

He made a funny face.

They rarely greeted each other, and now she was acting out of character.

"Is someone coming over?" he asked.

"Nope. I just felt like making lasagna. We haven't sat down for a meal together in so long, I thought it would be nice."

"I had dinner on the plane."

"You can make room for this."

Dean sniffed the air. "I suppose I can. Why aren't you out with friends?"

"Are you trying to get rid of me?" Lydia forced a smile, and then turned around and put the noodles in boiling water. She wanted to slap herself for the poor choice of words.

"You usually have plans."

Lydia turned around and held up some vegetables. "Want to help? Or would you rather settle in?" She turned to the fridge and asked, "Do you want a beer?"

He gave her a funny look. "Thanks."

Why was she being so helpful? He would definitely know something was wrong.

"I think I'll just turn the news on. I'll just get in your way." He went over to the couch, put his feet on the coffee table, and opened his drink.

Lydia made a face. He knew how much it irritated her when he put his feet up like that, but at least it gave her some space to pull herself together. She was freaked out and overcompensating.

She glanced at him, wondering if she could sneak over to his office and check the dates on his calendar. She needed to find out for sure if the dates lined up. Even though his attention was on the TV, she wouldn't be able to walk over without him noticing.

Her mind buzzed with questions while she made the side dishes as the lasagna baked. She was just glad to have kept him away from the bedroom for a while longer. With any luck, the smell of dinner would cover what was left of the perfume.

When the food was almost ready, she set the table. She found a bottle of red wine and put it next to Dean's plate. If nothing else, she would get him relaxed and sleepy so he wouldn't question her strange behavior. She would have to stay away from the wine so that she wouldn't get comfortable and say too much. That was her tendency when the wine came out.

"Dinner's ready."

Dean rose and scanned the spread. "It looks delicious." He sat and filled his plate.

Lydia barely put anything on her plate, but he didn't seem to notice. "How was your trip?"

"Same old. Just working the whole time." He finished off the beer and poured the wine.

"You leave again tomorrow?" she asked.

Dean nodded and then swallowed. "This time to Chicago. Looks like a short trip. You might actually see me twice in one week."

"Imagine that."

He reached for bread and then took a sip of wine. "I didn't think I was hungry until I tasted your cooking. It's been too long."

She took a small bite. "What are you going to do in Chicago?"

"I might catch a Cubs' game."

"Oh? By yourself?" she asked.

His eyes widened and he cleared his throat. "Uh, no."

"Who, then?"

Dean took a big bite and then indicated that he couldn't speak.

Lydia wanted to ask more, but if she got too close to finding out if his guest had anything to do with the clippings, he might suspect something. She took a few bites, and they ate in silence.

"That was good," Dean said. "I don't usually get to eat anything like this." His eyes narrowed. "I hope you don't expect anything later. You know how tired I get after traveling. I just want to check my email and get to sleep. I have an early flight in the morning."

"Of course."

Dean wiped his mouth and then dropped the napkin on the plate. He rose and headed for his office.

Normally if Lydia had gone to the trouble of making them dinner, she would have been upset about him stonewalling her again. She was glad that he didn't suspect anything was wrong. She just had to get through until the next morning, and that shouldn't be too difficult so long as he didn't notice the perfume or a piece of glass she might have missed.

She heard the sound of his computer turning on, and her body relaxed. He would likely be in there for hours—he was much happier looking at the screen than at her. Her appetite returned and she was able to enjoy the food she prepared.

When she had everything cleaned up, Dean was still in his office glued to the computer. When would he leave so she could check out his calendar?

Lydia grabbed an organic ice cream bar and went out onto the deck.

She leaned against the railing, enjoying the warm evening air. She had always enjoyed summers in the Pacific Northwest.

Lydia looked across her neighbor's yard, and over to the park across the street. Children squealed and chased each other. Her heart ached. Not only for the days when she didn't have a care in the world, but also for the kids she and Dean would never have. It wasn't for a lack of trying, but not even modern medicine could help them.

All of that had put an enormous strain on their marriage, and that's when things started going downhill. Dean had offered to travel for work to bring in more money for the expensive procedures. Then after those failed, he traveled even more but spent the money on sports cars and additions to the home.

She had begged him to look into adoption, but he had been adamant that he didn't want to raise someone else's kid. Lydia had thought she could change his mind, but all she had done was push him away further. He traveled even more and answered his phone less.

That was when their marriage went from strained to a farce. They had started out adoring each other, but they weren't strong enough to handle the infertility.

Lydia ate the last bite of her bar and then leaned against the railing, still watching the kids. She imagined for a moment what it would be like to be one of the moms chasing after little ones. Some of them looked like they hadn't slept in days, while others looked pristine.

Which kind would she have been? Lydia looked down at herself, unable to imagine being one of the ragged ones. Though her love life was in shambles, she had everything else under control.

Loud laughter came from the other side of the yard. She looked over across the other side of her yard and saw a group of teenagers running down the street, spraying something all over each other.

Oh, to be that carefree. Could she ever get to that point again? Especially now, after learning Dean's secret? Lydia shook her head. She didn't know for sure that he had killed those women. She needed to do some digging, and stop assuming until she had more to go on.

The first thing she would do was go over the calendar in his office to check his destinations against the dates on the clippings. Lydia was pretty sure of what she would find, though. Why else would he hide them like that?

Maybe she did need a drink. More than anything, she wanted to believe the answer was something simpler. What if he was working as a private eye and just hadn't told her? He could have lost his job and been embarrassed about that.

That would make sense, because Dean had worked so hard to get where he was in the company. He would also make a good detective. The man could pick anything apart, and he wasn't afraid of anyone. He would ask questions no one else dared to speak.

Lydia looked down at their perfectly manicured lawn. She knew he hadn't switched jobs. They left messages on the voice mail every so often, and Lydia had seen their deposits into the bank account.

She had to be missing something.

Years ago, he had talked about writing a novel. He could have kept those articles for story ideas, but why would he go to all the trouble to hide them?

What if their whole life was a lie? Even though so many things sucked, there was a lot that was good too. Especially the money he made and let her spend. The more she spent, the better he looked. He loved bragging about all the nice things they had.

Despite everything they'd gone through, and his complete lack of interest in her, there was a part of her that still cared about him. She missed the fun guy he had been early on. The one who had showered her with flowers and handwritten poetry.

But if he really was murdering people, she would have to leave him. But could that really be what was going on? What if there was another reason for those clippings?

Her main objective needed to be finding out what was really going on with Dean. Then she would decide what to do from there. Whether she ran or went to the police, she would need solid evidence. Especially if she went to the authorities.

Once she had a chance, she would search for clues and when she found enough, she would take it to the police.

Lydia's stomach twisted in knots. How had her life come to this?

Snooping

LYDIA SAT UP, gasping for air. She looked around the room. It had only been a dream, but it felt so real. In the dream, Dean chased her through the house with a knife because she had accused him of killing those women.

Dean lay sprawled across his side of the bed, snoring.

"Are you awake?" she whispered.

He didn't answer, except to keep snoring. Maybe sleeping in the same bed hadn't been such a good idea. She hadn't wanted to throw off the routine and make him suspect anything.

Lydia pulled out the novel she had put the notes in and then slid out of bed. She carried the book downstairs to Dean's office and turned the light on. Setting the novel down, she took his calendar off the wall and flipped it back to January. There had been five killings this year, and if the dates matched, Lydia would search for last year's calendar to see if those lined up too.

She pulled the paper out and looked at the first date. January twenty-third in Detroit. Lydia scanned the calendar for the twenty-third, and sure enough, it was his last day in Detroit for that particular trip.

The next one was in Boston on the first of March. That was three days into his trip there.

San Diego on April twelfth…check.

Houston on May fifteenth.

Lydia's stomach churned acid, and the paper shook in her hand. She looked down and noticed her whole body trembled.

"I can't look at any more of this," Lydia muttered. Still shaking, she put the calendar back on the wall. Once it was straight, she grabbed her book and paper, and then went out into the living room. She grabbed a warm blanket and sat on the couch, staring at a wall.

What was she supposed to do now? Was it enough to go to the authorities? Probably not. She had no proof. They would probably laugh at her. She had seen enough crime scene shows to know her 'evidence' was circumstantial. Sure, he'd been in all of the cities at the times of the murders, but was there proof of him talking to any of the women?

If there was, that would take more digging, and she couldn't do that yet. It was all she could do to keep her dinner down.

Taking a deep breath, she tried to think of another explanation. Could he have been a spy, not allowed to speak of his work? That was doubtful, given how much he loved to boast.

Her stomach twisted in knots. Should she have seen this coming? Were there signs she had ignored all this time? He traveled a lot—far more than any other husband she knew of, but she shouldn't have suspected this. Affairs, sure. Lydia wasn't stupid. He hadn't slept with her in a long time, and she knew what that usually meant.

That was why she had fallen in love with someone else. Chad's marriage had been on the brink of divorce and they kept running into each other. Lydia had thought it was meant to be. Neither of their spouses liked them anymore, and they could talk for hours on end about everything and nothing.

Lydia had been so sure they would both divorce and end up together. But after Chad's daughter came up missing, and Lydia gave him all the space in the world, he had turned back into a family man. Her heart ached. Even after nearly a year, it hurt so much. She had let herself fall— and hard.

She wanted to talk with him and see what he thought about this. He had a sharp mind, and he would know exactly what to do. Lydia shook her head. Though she knew he still cared about her, they weren't speaking unless they ran into each other socially. Even then, it was as though they didn't have history together.

What about her friends? Bri probably couldn't handle this. When her next door neighbor suffered a break-in, Bri had nearly had a meltdown imagining someone coming into her house to butcher her in her sleep.

No. Lydia couldn't talk with her about this.

The other ladies wouldn't be much more help. Savannah was too focused on celebrity gossip, and wouldn't keep quiet. And Savannah was just as bad at spreading rumors. Cara was about to have a baby. Lydia couldn't tell her about this. That wouldn't be fair to her.

Lydia's family was too far, and this wasn't a conversation she could have over the phone or through email. She was going to have to handle this one on her own, at least for the time being.

Normal people didn't go on a killing rampage because their marriage hit some bumps in the road. There was no way she could have known that would be how he would react to their problems.

If this was how Dean dealt with stress, he had to have other underlying issues. Had she missed anything? He had a temper, sure. What guy didn't? She shuddered, remembering all the times she had hid in her closet with her mom or brother when her dad was in a rage.

Guys got angry when things didn't go their way. It's just the way it was. It was worse when alcohol was involved, but that didn't mean she should have known that her husband was killing people.

Lydia looked up at the time. Two hours had passed since she sat down. She would be better off going to bed so she could think clearly—assuming Dean didn't kill her in her sleep.

She folded the blanket back up and put it where it had sat since the weather warmed up. Then she tip-toed back into the bedroom and slid the book back into place before climbing into bed.

Dean rolled over and looked at her.

Lydia's heart sped up.

"Is everything okay?" he asked.

"Just had to go to the bathroom," Lydia lied.

"Okay." He closed his eyes and was snoring before Lydia's head hit the pillow.

Lydia pulled the covers up, forcing herself to breathe normally. She could see light poking through the window when she finally grew drowsy.

When Lydia woke up, the sun lit up the entire room and she had it to herself. Dean was probably downstairs at his computer before leaving to go to work. When did he say his flight out was? She couldn't remember. It was like the discovery had pushed everything else out of her mind.

What she really needed was to talk to someone. Nothing helped her to think straight like discussing what was on her mind. But she couldn't go to just anyone with this. What if she was wrong? She was accusing her husband of being a serial killer.

Or what if she was right, and someone who didn't believe her told Dean what she thought? The blood drained from her head. As much as she needed to talk to someone, she couldn't. Even if she did trust someone enough, it wasn't something she could just slide into conversation.

"Can you hand me a napkin? Oh, I think my husband is killing people. Pass the salt, please."

Lydia shook her head. She had to decide on one thing and stick with it. No more flip-flopping. It was time to pull herself together.

After he left for his next trip, she would have to go through everything. She would collect anything that could be proof. Receipts, notes, anything.

Dean came into the room, and Lydia jumped.

"What's going on with you?" he asked.

"I've been having bad dreams."

"You're not thinking about adopting again, are you?"

"What? No. Where did that come from? We haven't talked about that in a long time."

"Good. I just came up to let you know I have to go into the office before I go to the airport, so I'm leaving now."

"All right."

"See you in a couple days." Dean turned around and left the room. There was a time that such a brash goodbye would have hurt Lydia, but this time she was relieved to have him gone.

She leaned back on her pillow and closed her eyes. A couple days to figure out what to do. Would she be better off packing up and cutting her losses, or would it be better to stick around and look for clues?

If she just left, her conscience would bother her. What if he kept killing people, and she could have stopped it from happening? If she found enough evidence, she could take it to the cops and they could lock him away.

Lydia's phone buzzed on the nightstand. She picked it up and saw Bri's face on the screen.

"Hey, Bri."

"We missed you yesterday," Bri said in her best pout voice. "You're not going to stand us up today, are you? We're going to the beach, remember? You're bringing the wine."

"I'll be there." Maybe after spending some time in the sun with friends and good wine, she would be able to think clearly. As long as she kept a tight reign over her tongue while sipping. "See you in about an hour?"

"Perfect. Cara's saving our favorite spot."

"Ciao." Lydia ended the call and went to the window, opening the blinds and letting the sun warm her. She would sit on the beach and forget all about Dean for a while. "Dean who?" She smiled.

Lydia grabbed her favorite bikini, threw it on the counter, and got into the shower thinking of nothing other than a day on the warm sand. After putting on makeup and pulling her hair back, she threw on some cute shorts and tank top. Downstairs, she found a picnic basket a few of their best bottles of wine. Humming, she tucked in some wine glasses, and then looked around for anything else.

When she was sure she had everything, she slid on her favorite pair of flip flops, grabbed her best pair of sunglasses, and made her way to her car. It was going to be a good day.

Lydia pulled out of the garage and was about to close the door when she noticed something on the ground. Whatever it was fluttered from the draft created as she moved the car. She stopped and got out. It looked like a piece of paper.

She bent down to pick it up. It was a page from a newspaper. Lydia started to fold it closed when she noticed one of the headlines.

Restaurant manager found dead.

Lydia stared at it for a moment before scanning for a date. Three days earlier.

Forgetful

LYDIA STOOD IN the middle of Dean's office, staring at his massive desk. She wanted to know what was in the top drawer. The one he kept locked at all times. Even when they got along, he never opened it in front of her.

She didn't have the key, nor did she know where it was, so she left it alone and turned her attention toward the things she had access to. She needed to gather whatever additional information she could, and she didn't have a lot of time before meeting with the girls.

Her heart pounded so hard, she feared it would burst right out of her chest.

Lydia took a few deep breaths and then decided to start with the file cabinets. He had two of them, one on either side of the desk. She started with the top drawer of the closest one. Heavy, it resisted her efforts to open it. With a mighty tug, the drawer snapped open. She ran her fingers over the tops of the files, looking at the scribblings.

They all appeared to be bills collected over the years. Nothing remotely interesting—unless he hid anything under the guise of something so ordinary. She pulled out the one marked as the cable bill for two years earlier.

Going through all the papers—twice—she saw nothing other than statements with "paid," written in Dean's handwriting. She put them back in the file and carefully put it back from where she had taken it. Then she grabbed one for the cell phones from a few years back. It was the same thing. Nothing unusual.

After looking through about a dozen more, she sat on his chair, tired. If he'd gone to so much trouble hiding the clippings under a floorboard beneath the heavy safe, would he really leave any evidence somewhere as obvious as his file cabinet?

Sighing, she pulled open a random drawer from the desk on the left side. It was full of loose papers.

Lydia picked up a stack and flipped through them. Her heart skipped a beat. They were all from the cell phone carrier, and they were printouts of *her* activity. She didn't find one with Dean's.

She flipped through the stack, looking at the dates. They went back before she started seeing Chad. Her stomach dropped to the floor. Did Dean know everything? Had he been paying extra close attention to her every move, even when he acted like she didn't exist?

Shaking, she flipped through the pages—and there were a lot of them since she loved talking with her friends so much. She saw call after to call to not only her friends, but Chad as well. Some of the first few to Chad had little tick marks next to them, but none of the rest did.

Did that mean he'd taken notice of a new number and then looked into it? All he would have had to do was call it and pretend to have a wrong number. He knew about her affair.

Lydia dropped the papers onto the floor, sending them scattering in all directions.

Her stomach lurched. She ran to the nearest bathroom and threw up. As she cleaned herself up, she realized it wasn't that big of a deal. Or at least that's what she told herself.

Dean had started his affairs long before she had her one, and she'd had better proof than just a call log. That one day when she was doing laundry and found unfamiliar women's underwear stuck inside of one of his shirts—that was all the proof she needed. Not only were they not hers, but they were two sizes bigger.

He couldn't have tried to talk his way out of it if he'd wanted to. She never would have fit into them. He couldn't have said anything to explain his way out of that.

She'd thought about confronting him at the time, but they weren't even on speaking terms then. So she had stuck them in a plastic bag and hid them in a hiding spot of her own in the laundry room—a place he would never accidentally find anything.

Lydia went back into Dean's office and picked up the papers from the floor. She made sure they were all in the right order before returning them to the cabinet. As she slid the drawer closed, she thought she heard something from another part of the house.

She froze, listening.

The front door closed. She knew that sound because it stuck a bit, making a different noise than any of the other doors. Her eyes widened as she slid the drawer closed the rest of the way.

If Dean had come back home, she wouldn't be able to leave his office unseen. And it would be the first place he came—but why would he return home?

Footsteps sounded on the hardwood floors. He was heading right for her.

Pulse on fire, she stood and pretended to look in the file.

"Lydia. What are you doing here?"

She looked up at him, careful to keep her voice steady. "I didn't hear you come in. I was looking for a statement."

He raised an eyebrow and looked around. "Why didn't you call me?"

Lydia thought quickly. "I heard about a great deal that could save us a lot of money. I wanted to see if I was right."

Dean narrowed his eyes. "I told you not to worry about the bills. It's my thing."

"But it could save us money."

"I don't care. How many times do I have to tell you I don't want you in my office?"

"Sorry. Aren't you going to be late for your flight?" she asked.

"No. It's been delayed, and I forgot something."

Lydia closed the cabinet drawer. "I'll get out of your way." She moved out of his way, and then a paper underneath his desk caught her attention. It looked like one of the papers she'd dropped.

She looked back at him. It didn't appear that he could see it from his angle.

"What did you forget?" she asked, trying to distract him.

He turned to her, furrowing his eyebrows. "What's been going on with you?"

"Wh…what do you mean?" she asked.

"You've been nice ever since I got home. You even made me dinner. What's going on?"

"I just thought…maybe we could try again, you know."

"Try what?" he demanded.

Lydia swallowed. "You know. Our marriage. Neither one of us is happy."

"You should be. There isn't a thing you lack. If you want something, it's yours. You don't even have to work."

"I couldn't even if I wanted to." She studied his expression, trying to see if he flinched. He didn't.

She had a secret part-time job working for a magazine under a pen name. It was fun and gave her a way to send some extra money to her sick mother who she almost never got to see. As far as she knew, Dean knew nothing about the magazine column or any of the money associated with it.

He stepped forward, glaring at her. "Why would you want a job? You get to play with your pampered friends all day without a worry in the world."

"What if I did want to?" she asked. "You wouldn't let me, would you?"

"Of course not! *My* wife isn't going to work. You want a job? Fire your housekeeper and clean everything yourself."

Lydia shook her head, tears threatening. She had to keep herself together. "You know that's not what I want to do."

"And that's exactly why I allow the maid. So you don't have to do menial work."

"That's not the kind of work I want—"

"Enough." Dean's nostrils flared. "This discussion is over. I came home to grab a paper, not be lambasted by you."

"I'm not trying to—"

"I said enough, Lydia." He walked by her and opened one of the drawers in his desk.

She watched him, internally begging him not to see the paper she'd dropped.

He turned around. "What are you still doing in here? Get out of my office. I don't want to have to lock it, but I will if it comes to that."

Nodding, Lydia backed up until she was out into the hall.

Dean stepped out of the office, closing the door. "Do I have your word that you'll stay out?"

She nodded.

"I need to hear you say it."

"I'll stay out."

"What were you doing in there, really?" He stepped closer to her.

"Looking for our cell phone payment."

Dean moved closer. Lydia could smell his aftershave.

He raised an eyebrow. "I don't think so."

Lydia backed up, but bumped into a wall. "I was."

"I saw the paper on the floor, Lyds." He took another step. Their noses nearly touched.

"Like I told you," she said. "Cell phone records. Those were just phone calls, so I put them away. I needed to know how much we're paying."

"Again, I'll remind you to let me handle the bills. If you want to look into a new carrier or plan, just ask me."

"Okay."

"Basically, I don't want you so much as thinking about anything that involves the both of us without asking me first. If I don't approve it, you don't think it."

"Sorry, Dean." She didn't mean it, but usually, apologizing would get him to back off.

He stepped back, running hands through his hair. "I don't have time to worry about you. I have more important things to focus on."

Lydia looked him in the eyes. "You can trust me."

"I'd better be able to. Or you'll regret it."

She jumped.

"Good. I finally got your attention."

Lydia just stared at him, unable to find her voice.

"Look. I have to get going, or I really will miss my plane. If you have any questions, just call. Leave a message. You know how busy I get. Text

21

me if you want. Just don't go through my stuff. I have it organized the way I do for a reason, and I don't want it messed with—and I can always tell when it has been."

Lydia nodded, fully understanding the threat.

"Good. Now stay out of my office."

"I will."

He backed up, and Lydia finally took a normal breath.

Beach

BRI STEVENS ROLLED over on the beach blanket, looking at the bright blue, cloudless, Pacific Northwest sky. She flipped her long blonde hair behind her so it wouldn't mess up her tan. "Where's Lydia? She should've been here by now."

"Oh, you know her," Savannah Jackman said, pulling her dark, curly hair behind her. "Late and great." She spread out her own blanket and sat down, grabbing sunscreen from her bag.

"Why do you bother with that stuff?" Bri asked. "You're not going to burn. You've got that dark, gorgeous skin."

Savannah wrinkled her nose. "I still burn. I just don't look like a lobster like you when I do. Don't we go over this every summer?"

"I still wouldn't bother." Bri grabbed the bottle from Savannah and squeezed some onto her hand.

"Seriously," Savannah said, her dark eyes glaring at Bri. "You're husband's darker than me and he uses sunblock."

Bri shrugged, rolling her big, blue eyes playfully. "Doesn't mean I would."

Cara Ross moved her blanket closer to the shade. "I should've brought an umbrella." She looked at Bri. "Did you remind Lydia to bring me something nonalcoholic?"

Bri reached over and rubbed Cara's belly. "I'm sure she remembered. You never let us forget you can't drink. You know what? You're lucky, Cara. You're at the cute stage in the summer. With both of my girls, I was enormous during the summer."

"Where are the kids now?" Cara asked, scooting out of Bri's reach.

"Summer camp again this year. It's a win-win. They have fun, and I get to have a life, too." Bri showed off her big, beautiful smile that she knew made every woman jealous and every man melt.

"Oh, there's Lyds," Savannah said, pointing toward the parking lot. "And it looks like she has a lot of bottles sticking out of her basket. I'm sure one is just for you, Cara."

"I hope so. All I brought was water." Cara pulled her long, straight, naturally red hair into a ponytail.

"Do you have sunblock?" Bri asked. "You're the one who really needs it between those freckles and being pregnant."

"I lathered up before I left." Cara moved closer to the shade again.

Bri shook her head. The poor thing was going to have a hard day at the beach. She wouldn't have been surprised if Cara ended up leaving early. Bri turned and saw Lydia had almost reached their little spot. Bri waved, not getting up. The sun was too comfortable, relaxing her.

Lydia dumped her picnic basket on the ground, sending sand flying.

"Watch out," Savannah said, brushing it off her blanket. "You're going to make it stick to our sunblock."

"Sorry." Lydia looked distracted as she shook out her blanket.

"Are you okay, Lyds?" asked Bri.

Lydia smiled. "Of course. Why?"

Bri shrugged. "You just don't look yourself today."

"Dean was home last night, right?" Cara asked.

"Oh," Savannah said. "That explains it. Was he being a jerk?"

Lydia pulled the wine glasses out of her basket. "No more than usual. Should we start with white?"

"I was hoping for red," Savannah said, "but whatever."

"Do you have anything without spirits?" asked Cara, looking annoyed.

Lydia pulled out a smaller bottle. "You think I'd forget about Cara Ross and her sweet little baby? Pomegranate apple cider just for you." Lydia handed Cara the bottle, smiling.

"I told you she wouldn't forget," Bri said. She turned to Lydia. "White wine sounds good to me. Want me to open it?"

Soon they were all sipping from their glasses, discussing celebrity drama. Bri kept looking back at Lydia. She wasn't into the conversation as much as usual. She usually knew more gossip than anyone else, but today she didn't even seem interested. Between that and missing yesterday's outing with the girls, Bri knew something was up. "You sure you're okay, sweetie?"

"I'm just tired," Lydia said. "Dean kept me up with his snoring."

"It's horrible," Cara agreed. Then she added quickly, "Men's snoring, that is. I hate it when Ethan snores all night. Sounds like a hog in heat."

Bri raised an eyebrow at Cara. Now she thought about it, Cara wasn't acting like herself. What was going on with their little group?

"I'm just saying," Cara said. "So, do you guys wanna see the new Donatello Williams movie? He's super hot in the previews."

Savannah fanned herself. "You're not kidding. Let's see it this week. Did you see those cutoffs he wore in the chase scene on the train?"

"Don't remind me," Cara said. "I nearly drooled all over myself during the commercial."

They made plans, but Bri couldn't get her mind off either Lydia or Cara. What was going on with them?

"Right, Bri?" asked Savannah.

Bri turned to her. "What?"

"I said all men snore."

"Back to that? Not Corey," Bri said. "He's perfect."

"You two make me sick," Cara said. "Together all those years and still in love. It's just not right."

"Like you and Ethan aren't still crazy about each other."

Cara rolled her eyes and shook her head.

"No?" Bri asked. "When did this happen?"

"No marriage is perfect," Cara snapped. "Except for Bri and Corey. But then again, if I was married to Corey Stevens, I'd do whatever he wanted. That man is the walking, talking definition of hot. Has he aged since you two married?"

"Yes, but he's like a fine wine," Bri said, taking a sip of freshly poured wine. "He just gets better with time."

"That he does," Savannah agreed. "He and Tom, both. My Tom ages, he just does it well. I love how the lines around his eyes crinkle when he laughs. Makes my heart stop."

"Can we stop talking about how perfect your husbands are?" Cara asked. "We get it. Tom and Corey are not only perfect, but hot, too. You can stop bragging already."

Bri sat up. "You have nothing to complain about. Ethan is—"

"What's eating you?" Savannah asked, glaring at Cara.

"Probably hormones," Bri said. "Or is Ethan turned off by the pregnancy?"

Cara's mouth formed a straight line and her face turned red.

"Bri," Savannah exclaimed. She elbowed Bri.

"It happens. It's nothing personal—don't feel bad if that's the case. Some guys are just built that way. Just how they're wired."

"Is Corey?" snapped Cara.

"No. He thought it was beautiful that I was growing a new life." Bri smiled, remembering the way he would caress her stomach. "He adored me."

Savannah sighed. "He would. If I didn't have Tom, I'd be so jealous."

Cara got up and moved her blanket over. "The shade keeps moving. We should've picked a different spot."

Lydia stood. "I've got an umbrella in my trunk. I'll get it."

"I am the only one who thinks something's wrong with her?" Bri asked.

"Cara?" Savannah asked, looking at a strand of dark hair.

"No." Cara shoved Savannah. "She meant Lydia."

Savannah looked at another strand of hair. "My hairdresser isn't getting a tip next time. She totally didn't get the highlights bright enough." She pulled her hair back into a bun. "Anyway, yeah, Lydia's being way too quiet. Do you know what's up?"

"No," Bri said, "but I'm going to find out."

"You want to know what I think?" Savannah asked, leaning back.

"What?" Cara asked, not looking amused.

Savannah slid off her shades. "The girl needs to get laid."

"Wow, Savannah. Why don't you tell us what you really think?" Bri asked, shaking her head.

"Grow up," Cara said.

"You can't tell me you weren't thinking it too," Savannah said. "Dean hasn't gone near her in, what, years? Maybe she should try to rekindle what they used to have. They were cute before things went south."

"Are you for real?" Cara asked, glaring at Savannah.

"Why wouldn't I be? They're married."

Cara rolled her eyes. "You call that a marriage?"

"What about the guy she was seeing?" Bri asked. "Maybe she can work things out with him again."

Savannah shook her head. "I think she would if she could. She's still stuck on him."

Bri looked toward the parking to see if Lydia was getting close. "You really think so?"

"Yeah," Savannah said. "She was head over heels for him. I can't believe she never told any of us who he was. Or did she tell one of you?"

"Not me," Cara said, inching over into the shade again.

"Me neither," Bri said. "And believe me, it wasn't for a lack of trying. All I got was that he was married, too, and she didn't want to say his name. She didn't want to ruin his reputation."

"She thought he was going to leave his wife, right?" Savannah asked.

Bri nodded. "Too bad he didn't. I really wanted to meet him. He sounded almost as wonderful as Corey."

"Oh, here she comes," Cara said. "I'm so glad she has an umbrella."

Lydia joined them and set up the umbrella for Cara.

"So, what did you do yesterday?" Savannah asked Lydia. "We missed you."

"I missed you girls, too." Lydia gave a weak smile. "Something came up at the house and I had to fix it. It's no big deal."

"Are you sure?" Bri asked.

"What is this, twenty questions?" Lydia frowned.

"Sorry." Bri tried to read Lydia's expression, but came up empty.

Cara poured herself more cider. "So, how about the Mariners? I heard they won again last night."

Savannah rolled her eyes at Cara.

Someone's cell phone rang.

"That's me." Savannah sat up and dug into her bag. "It's Tom." She slid her finger across the screen. "Hi, babe. What's up? … You did? …

Yeah, I'll join you. Just give me a few minutes. Love you." She slid her finger across the screen and threw it back in her bag. "He got off early and the shop is done with his Harley. We're going to go riding. Sorry to bail on you girls, but I can't pass that up."

"And you shouldn't." Bri tossed some sand at her. "Have fun."

Lydia stood. "I'm going to get going, too. I just remembered something I need to do." She looked at Cara. "You can hang onto the umbrella. Just bring it next time or whatever."

Bri looked into Lydia's beautiful, dark eyes. "Girlfriend, if you need to talk, give me a call."

"Sure."

They said their goodbyes as Savannah and Lydia took off.

Cara and Bri both got comfortable on their blankets, watching the light waves splash on the shore.

"I don't know how you can stay in the sun so long," Cara said. "Even when I'm not pregnant, I can't be in the sun as much as you."

"It's a gift." Bri flipped herself over. "Do you have any ideas what's bugging Lydia?"

Cara looked away. "Nope. I'm sure she'll get over it." She twisted a strand of her red hair.

"Why are you so angry today? Seems like every time we mention Lydia you act like you swallowed a spider." Bri ran a finger through the sand next to her blanket.

"She just annoys me. Don't you get tired of her whiny voice? Or how she thinks the world revolves around her? Ugh."

"She's not whiny," Bri said, staring into Cara's green eyes. "And she brought cider and an umbrella for you. What did you bring for her?"

Cara sighed. "She's trying to cover up the fact that she hates me."

"Lydia hates you?" Bri asked. "As if. We've all been tight for years. If she had something against you, she would have told one of us, and she hasn't said a word."

"Did you stop to think that her acting weird is because of me?" Cara asked.

"No." Bri picked some lint off her blanket. "She's always adored you. Remember when you guys almost lost your house and she dropped everything and helped you set up a garage sale to pay your mortgage that month? She even donated some of her jewelry."

Cara's face turned pale. "I nearly forgot about that. All the more reason for her to hate me."

"What would she have against you? I've never heard her utter a negative thing about you."

"Well...." Cara took a deep breath. She swallowed and then played with a nail, still looking pale.

"What?" Bri's eyes widened. "What are you keeping from me?"

Cara picked at a nail, but wouldn't look at Bri. "I might have done something that would piss her off. Big time. Like, enough to make her hate me forever."

"What? She wasn't angry. We'd all know if she was. Lydia was...I don't know. Sad? What did you do?"

Cara looked away, not saying anything.

"Would you just spill it?" Bri asked. "What did you do?"

Cara put a hand on her belly and looked at Bri.

Bri stared at her, waiting.

"This baby...."

"Yes?" asked Bri.

"It's Dean's."

Bri's eyes widened. She couldn't have heard Cara correctly. It wasn't possible.

"I've finally left you speechless."

"You didn't. Tell me you didn't sleep with Lydia's husband. You and Lydia are so close, too."

Cara shook her head. "It's his."

"But, but you and Ethan were trying to have a baby. How do you know it's Dean's? And when did this happen?" Bri demanded.

"You know how after a year I wanted to get tested to see if we had any medical reasons for not getting pregnant?"

"Yeah."

"Well, we did. Ethan was out of town when they called with the results. Basically, he's shooting blanks. There's no chance of getting pregnant by him. I was in tears, and went to talk to Lydia. I knew she'd understand after everything she went through with Dean. Anyway, she wasn't home, but Dean was. He saw how upset I was and insisted that I come inside until I was fit to drive." Cara bit her lip. "One thing led to another, and now here I am." She looked down at her belly.

Bri couldn't believe her ears. "You didn't tell Ethan about his, uh, issue?"

"Nope. I didn't know how to tell him, and I was riddled with guilt for betraying both him and Lyds. A few weeks passed, and I realized I was about a week late."

"Does Dean know?"

Tears filled her eyes. "It's complicated."

"Complicated?" Bri exclaimed. "Either he does or he doesn't."

"I'll explain it later."

"Have you seen Dean since then?" asked Bri.

Cara bit her lip again. "Maybe."

"Cara, Cara. What were you thinking? I thought you were riddled with guilt?"

"It's hard to feel guilty when Ethan thinks I'm disgusting."

"Oh, come on. He might not be as attracted to you as usual, but disgusting? You're still gorgeous, and rocking that bikini, might I add."

"Disgusting was the word he used," Cara said. "I've put on weight everywhere, and he doesn't like it."

"Some men are so stupid. But then again, so are you."

"What?" asked Cara. "Me?"

"Dean's one of your best friend's husbands. And it sounds like you've seen him more than just that one time."

"He's the baby's father."

"And he's also Lydia's husband." Bri felt defensive for Lydia.

Cara squirmed. "I know, but Lyds only stays with him for the money. It's like Savannah said, they haven't been together in years."

Bri arched an eyebrow.

"You're not going to say anything to her." It wasn't a question.

"Not if I want you keeping my secret safe." Bri took a sip of wine, guilt riddling her.

"That's right," Cara said. "You know it would cost your marriage."

Bri stared at Cara, anger replacing the guilt. How could she have ever thought Cara was a good friend when she held this over her head? Bri thought back through everything their little group had been through over the last few years. They'd all rallied around Lydia when she had fertility problems and then when Dean started traveling and they first suspected his cheating. When Savannah was injured after a car accident, they had all come together to help take care of her while Tom worked. And then when Corey had been dragged into a lengthy court battle, all the girls banded together to help Bri and Corey out.

Could their group ever be the same again? And how could she possibly keep something like this from Lydia?

Digging

THE DOORBELL RANG. Lydia shoved the newspaper page between the wall and the couch, afraid Dean would catch her reading the article. It took her a moment to realize that he wouldn't have rung the doorbell.

"Pull yourself together," she told herself. She checked to make sure the paper wasn't sticking out, and then went to the front door to see who was there. She wasn't expecting anyone.

Hopefully, it wasn't the kid down the street asking her to subscribe to his newspaper route again. She always felt guilty about saying no, but they didn't read the paper.

At least not the local paper.

Lydia looked through the peephole and saw Bri smiling at her. She appeared to be holding something. Lydia opened the door and forced a smile. "Hey there. I didn't expect to see you."

Bri's smile widened. "You seemed down earlier, so I thought I'd surprise you with dinner." She held up a bag with the name of their favorite sushi place.

Lydia wasn't in the mood for company, but sushi did sound good, and she couldn't keep pushing Bri off. She knew something was up. Lydia would have to come up with something that sounded legit. "Sounds delicious."

"I got your favorites." Bri walked past, and Lydia heard her set the bags on the counter and pull out dishes.

"Thanks for thinking of me," Lydia called as she locked the door. She went into the kitchen and pulled out silverware.

"Well, Corey hates sushi, so I'm not being entirely selfless." Bri laughed. She flipped some of her long, blonde hair behind her shoulders and then doled out the food onto the two plates.

They carried everything to the table. They began eating in silence. Bri looked at Lydia, obviously expecting her to talk. Lydia had no intentions of sharing her news with anyone, not even—or especially?—her best friends.

"Anything you want to talk about?" Bri asked.

"Not really." Lydia stuffed a large bite into her mouth.

"Where's Dean off to this time?"

Lydia tried to remember where he said he was going. Had he said? Everything was such a blur since discovering those papers. "I can't remember. It's always somewhere."

"Still think he's cheating?"

"You think he's not?" Lydia asked. "He won't go near me."

"What about your mystery guy? You never told us much about him, but you were really happy when you two were together."

"Like I said before, he worked things out with his wife. They had a family emergency and then realized they needed to work together. Basically, she realized what she had just before she lost it."

"Sucks for you."

"Yep." Lydia finished off the wine in her glass.

"Anyone else interesting? Someone who's available?"

She couldn't deal with this conversation while thinking about the clippings. Maybe talking about it with Bri would help. Lydia opened her mouth to say something, but closed it. She couldn't bear to say the words.

"What?" Bri asked, looking curious.

Lydia shook her head.

"Well, we've got to make that our project. Time to find a good look-ing, *single* guy who's man enough to keep our Lydia happy."

"Easy as pie." Lydia tried to force a smile, but wasn't sure her mouth even twitched. Thinking about Chad made her feel even worse. They would have been together had he and Alyssa not worked things out. They had even been talking in detail about what kind of house they wanted. He even asked about her taste in rings—specifically what she liked and didn't like about her wedding ring.

"You really liked him," Bri said, bringing Lydia back to the present.

"I still love him. I can't let go, even though he's not coming back."

"It's been a year, sweetie."

"You don't have to tell me."

"It's time to move on."

Lydia wanted to say, *You have no idea.* The farther away from Dean she could get, the better.

"If he worked it out with his wife that long ago, he's not coming back."

"I know." That came out harsher than Lydia meant. "I just haven't met anyone. Do I need to have a guy at all times? Am I that pathetic?"

"Not at all. Do you want to move on? Or do you think there's a chance he'll return?"

"Maybe I just need some time to myself. I certainly get enough of that sharing a house with Dean."

Bri put her hand on top of Lydia's. "You're better than both of them. Maybe tomorrow we can look for—"

"I'm going to stick around here tomorrow."

"What about that new Donatello Williams movie? We'll look then."

"No single guy with a job is going to be at the movie theater on a weekday afternoon."

"We'll go in the evening, then."

"I'm not ready for this. It happened naturally last time. We kept running into each other—he playfully accused me of following him. We had a good laugh, and since it was lunchtime, I suggested we eat. We laughed and talked the whole time. There wasn't even a slight lull in the conversation. You can't force something like that, a real connection."

"We need to do something. I've never seen you so mopey. Is it the anniversary of your breakup or something?"

Lydia looked at the calendar. Actually, it was close to the date of the last time she and Chad had connected. Lydia had driven by the park and saw him there alone, and not at all dressed for being at the park. She thought something was wrong, and she'd been right. He had broken down sobbing. She held him in her arms and he cried.

Even as they had sat there, she knew somehow that was the last time they would really spend any time together.

Lydia squeezed her fists. The early summer was turning into a time of bad memories. First that, and now finding out about Dean.

She looked back to Bri. "Something like that."

Bri's face lit up. "I know. The HOA is having another meeting soon. I heard the old Jefferson house was bought by a single guy. I'll bet we can meet him there."

"He's probably gay." Lydia rested her chin on her hands.

"We need to work on your attitude."

"Seriously. Did you see what he did to the front yard? It's gorgeous."

"He probably hired someone. You're the only one around here who actually likes pruning rose bushes."

Lydia shrugged. "It's relaxing."

"Says you. Well, you're probably right about staying away from him. If you leave, you don't want to be in the same neighborhood as Dean. Awkward."

Or dead.

"Oh, I know." Bri's eyes lit up. "We could go to a club or a bar. Lots of single guys there."

"Why are you making me your latest project?"

Bri looked hurt. "I just care. We need to pull you out of this funk, Lyds. I knew something was wrong, and I was right. We need to fix this."

"You mean you need to fix me." Her gaze wandered over to the couch where that paper was hidden. Dean was on a short trip, and she had to decide if she would even be home when he got back.

"No, you don't need fixing. We just need to get your focus changed. Mystery man is out of the picture and Dean doesn't appreciate you. Time to find someone who does. What type are you into?"

Lydia slid her hands over her face. She loved Bri, but couldn't wait for her to leave.

"If I knew who the mystery man is, I would have a much better idea of your type. Is he handsome like Dean, or hot like Corey?"

Lydia poured more wine into her glass and took another long drink. "Neither. And his looks aren't what's important. It's the connection, you know? We could talk about anything, and even mundane tasks were fun because we were together."

"So he's an uggo?"

Lydia laughed despite herself. "No, definitely not."

"He is hot. I knew it." Bri nodded knowingly. "And I got you to laugh. Do I know him?"

"I'm never giving up his identity."

"You're still attached to him. You've got to let go. It's time to live your life."

"I think I need to figure out what I want for me first."

"You can still date while you do that."

"What would Dean think of you setting me up with someone?" Lydia was trying to change the subject.

"Do you really think he would care?" Bri gave Lydia a look of pity. "You always say he's got someone in every city he goes to."

"He obviously keeps me around for something."

Lydia got up and put the dishes in the sink. "Are you staying?"

"I came here to give you a girls' night."

"You pick the movie and I'll make popcorn." Lydia did her best to act normal while they watched the movie. She couldn't stop thinking about the piece of paper behind the couch, not that Bri would know what it meant. Dean was the one she needed to worry about. Why had he been so careless to leave it in the garage? It almost felt like a trap.

If Lydia put it with the others, he would know that he hadn't put it there. If she put it back in the garage, he would know she had seen it. If she attempted to sneak it back into his car, he would know it was placed there. He was careful about everything, and he was sure to have already realized it was missing, and would have gone through the entire car before going to the airport.

That paper might just be her undoing. She couldn't stop thinking about it. Maybe she needed to just burn it. Then he would have to wonder what happened to it, but never know. If it stayed in the house, he would eventually find it.

Lydia's stomach twisted in knots. She almost wanted to ask him about the clippings, to give him the chance to tell her something else other than what she had concluded. Maybe he was playing private eye, following someone. It was possible that he was keeping an eye on a coworker who traveled with him frequently.

The murders were more than a month apart, and they weren't every time he traveled somewhere.

Bri laughed, and Lydia realized she hadn't been paying attention to the movie at all. She couldn't keep living like this—obsessing over the papers. She needed to do something. What, though? Confront Dean, a possible serial killer? If so, he wouldn't bat an eye at getting rid of her.

Could she hire a private detective? It would be difficult to sneak out that much money without Dean noticing. He would demand to know what she had spent the money on.

She could move out and divorce him, but that didn't guarantee her safety. Her pulse raced. There wasn't enough time to process everything and take action before Dean returned. But if she really did believe he was guilty—did she?—then she would be stupid to stick around.

On the other hand, Dean had been collecting the clippings for over a year. He hadn't touched her in all of that time, not lovingly but also not roughly, either.

Maybe that was Lydia's answer. She needed to just relax—clear her head. There had to be another explanation. Her husband, a serial killer? No. It was more likely that Lydia was a bored housewife who had seen too many crime dramas.

Wasn't it?

Feelings

LYDIA ENDED THE call and threw her phone on the bed. She'd been making call after call to people she could find who were related to the murder victims. It was hard enough to find phone numbers in the first place, and most of the people she talked with didn't want to discuss details with a stranger.

She picked up the newest clipping, and it shook in her hand. Why hadn't she burned it? Dean was due back any time and she still had it. Part of her wanted to ask him about it. Act innocent but watch his reaction. It wasn't as though he would reach into his pocket and stab her for asking about a paper.

There was a coupon on the back for a sporting goods store. She'd been toying with using that as her angle. Hand the page to him coupon-side up. *Are you getting back into golf?* It was all she had. The only way to figure out if he had an alibi. Unless she was going to ask him straight out, but she was too chicken to do that.

Even if he were innocent, just asking if he had killed anyone would be enough for him to send her packing. She didn't have anywhere to go, not locally, where she wanted to continue living. Aside from that, he would find something in the prenup to keep from giving her any money. He would likely even keep her car. He had put it in his name so he could claim it as a business expense.

Lydia's palms grew sweaty despite the air conditioning. Her stomach heaved. She was going to throw up again, so she put the paper on the kitchen table, coupon-side up, and ran to the bathroom.

When she came out of the bathroom, she heard the garage door opening. Terror ran through her. Her feet moved before she could think. She ran to the fridge and grabbed a bottle of water, and then she went outside onto the porch acting as nonchalant as she could.

Lydia leaned against the railing at such an angle that she could see inside from the corner of her eye. She sipped the water while soaking up the sun. Dean wouldn't think anything of that.

He came inside, set his bags in front of his office, and went in there. He hadn't even glanced over at the table or Lydia outside. She let out a sigh of relief, and then went back inside.

Dean poked his head out of the office at the sound of the sliding glass door closing.

"Oh, you're home." Lydia made sure to sound surprised.

"It was a short trip, remember?"

"That's right. Well, tonight there's a HOA meeting. You should come. Everyone always asks about you. Some of the neighbors haven't even met you."

Dean groaned. "You know how I feel about those meetings."

"It's not a bunch of old biddies. There will be refreshments and wine. Maybe even some beer, depending on what other husbands are there."

"I really would rather relax after a long flight, Lydia."

"That's what you always say. Come on. You haven't seen Corey or Ethan in a long time."

Dean grimaced. "Did you ever think there's a reason for that?"

"Why live in a housing development if you're never going to see the neighbors?"

"If you leave me alone the rest of the day, I'll go."

"Deal." Lydia walked by him, and then stopped. "Oh, and I found some coupon you dropped in the garage. I put it on the table."

"Coupon?" he asked. Dean went over to the table and picked up the paper. Color drained from his face. "Right. I forgot about the coupon. Thanks."

"Sure," Lydia said, forcing enthusiasm. "Be ready to leave just before seven."

"Fine." He stared at the paper.

Lydia walked slowly away, keeping her focus on him. He held the clipping, staring at it. It shook in his hand.

"I'll grab takeout later. Are you in the mood for anything special?" she asked.

"What?" He looked up at her, his eyes wide. "Oh, sure. Whatever you want."

Lydia went upstairs and collapsed on the bed. That was not the reaction she was hoping for—he looked guilty. He was shaken by the paper. Who got upset over a coupon? No, it was because of the other ones hidden underneath the floorboard in their closet, all of which matched the dates of his travels.

Would he believe she was clueless? He was probably going to start watching her more closely to see if she knew or suspected anything. Lydia closed her eyes, focusing on her breathing. She had to be calm and act natural. Going to the meeting later was probably the best thing they could do.

She could watch him interact with others. It wasn't something she got to see often. She felt drowsy, and gave into it.

A hand on her arm woke her. Lydia's eyes popped open, and Dean stood next to the bed actually touching her. "What's going on?"

"It's almost seven. Time for your meeting. We can just eat there. You said they have refreshments, right?"

Why had he woken her? He would have loved nothing more than for her to sleep through the meeting so he wouldn't have to go. She sat up. "Yeah. I didn't mean to fall asleep. I was going to get dinner."

He smiled and she relaxed. He always had such a nice smile. It had actually been one of the first things that drew her to him. "Don't worry about it. I lost track of time myself." He took her hand and helped her up. "What should I wear? I have no idea what people wear to these things."

Lydia looked him over. "You're fine. Are those new slacks?"

"They were a Christmas gift from my parents. I just forgot about them for a while." He stared into her eyes.

Lydia's breath caught. What was going on? She cleared her throat. "Right. I remember you opening them. Well, I'd better get dressed. These are wrinkled from sleeping in them."

Dean stepped back, still looking at her. Lydia went into the closet and picked out a summer dress. She walked back into the room, and was surprised to see Dean still in there. He hadn't moved from where he had helped her off the bed.

They stared at each for a moment not saying anything. Lydia moved to the opposite side of the bed and set the dress down. Was he going to watch her get dressed? It was something she figured was normal in a typical marriage, but not for them.

He kept looking at her, and for a moment, Lydia felt exposed. But then she realized there was nothing he hadn't already seen—back when he had adored her. She didn't look any worse now. In fact, she looked better. She'd been eating mostly organic and had been working out more than ever.

She looked into his eyes. He could watch her and see what he'd been missing out on. Then he could remember that after she left him. Lydia wrapped her fingers around the bottom of her shirt and pulled it off slowly. She flung it into the laundry basket and looked back over at him.

His eyes were hungry, reminding her of the early days of their marriage. He walked over to her to and stood behind her, wrapping his arms around her. He was cold because he had his desk right under the AC unit in his office.

Chills ran through her, and goose bumps formed along Lydia's skin. Dean brushed her hair out of his way and she felt his lips on her neck, kissing toward her ear. She rolled her head to the side, giving him better access. Her muscles relaxed as warm familiarity enveloped her.

This was what their relationship had been like before it soured. Spontaneous shows of affection that always left her wanting more of him. She grabbed his hands and wrapped hers around them. He pressed his fingers against her skin harder as he kissed her earlobe, his breath sending more chills through her.

Could he be acting this way to get out of going to the meeting? Or to distract her from the clipping? Lydia shoved aside the thoughts, glad to be close to him in a way she'd wanted to be for so long.

Dean's hands moved toward her waist. "Let me help you with those shorts."

Lydia turned around, giving him easier access and then pulled his shirt off. She stared at him. She wasn't the only one who had been working out more. Lydia forced her lips on his and enjoyed every moment of reenacting their newlywed days.

It was as though they had gone back in time to their carefree days. She leaned against him as they lay in the bed, and he wrapped his arms around her.

"I think we're going to be late to your meeting." Dean pulled her closer. They fit together like they were made for each other.

"No complaints here." She caressed his arm, watching bumps form under the hair. She noticed some of them were silvery.

"What happens if you miss the meeting?"

Lydia turned to face him and ran her fingers along his strong jawline. "Just a fine."

"A fine? Really?"

"Yeah. They add it to the dues."

Dean kissed her nose. "I hope someone brings beer."

"Someone usually does."

He helped her off the bed, and as they got dressed. She walked by him into the bathroom, aware that his gaze lingered on her.

Dean came over to her and stood behind her. They stared at each other through the mirror. "Is it okay with you?" he asked. "Things haven't been…ideal lately."

Lydia stood taller. "Every marriage has its bumps."

He put his hands on her waist and spun her around. "It's time we moved past ours, don't you think?" His voice was husky.

"I do." Lydia stared into his eyes, noticing the lines around them were deeper than she was used to.

Dean ran his fingers through the length of her hair and then gave her a kiss, lingering. "We should get going before we end up with a late fee."

She nodded, her breath caught. He stepped away, and she watched as he walked out of the bathroom. Lydia took a deep breath and looked at herself in the mirror. What had just happened?

Was all that because of the newspaper? Did he realize his need for her, or was he merely going out of his way to make sure she was on his side? He knew everything she liked, so it would be easy enough for him to try to woo her back. And with her still broken over Chad, he was the perfect rebound. How ironic was that?

Meeting

LYDIA PRETENDED NOT to see the stares. Everyone was not only surprised to see Dean at the HOA meeting, but even more so that they were holding hands.

Bri raised an eyebrow at Lydia. The look on her face told Lydia that Bri wanted all the details as soon as possible.

Lydia turned around and made eye contact with Cara. She had a disapproving look on her face.

Dean squeezed her hand. "I'm going to grab a drink." He walked over to the beer and greeted some of the husbands standing near the table.

Bri made her way over to Lydia, and Savannah showed up from somewhere, too. They both stared at her, barely two inches from away.

"What's going on?" Savannah asked. "I've never seen Dean at one of these. I've barely seen him, period."

"I suggested he come, and he did. He seems to be in a good mood today."

Savannah raised an eyebrow. "You look a little flush. Just how good of a mood is he in?"

Lydia shoved her. "None of your business. Did you have a good motorcycle ride with Tom today?"

"None of my business?" Savannah laughed. "Sounds pretty good. Oh, yeah. We had a great ride. We went to…."

Lydia couldn't focus on what Savannah said, mostly because of the looks Bri was giving her. Lydia tried to ignore her, while pretending to be engaged with Savannah's story.

"What's up with Cara?" Lydia asked when Savannah was done.

"What do you mean?" Savannah asked. "She's fine."

"No," Lydia said. "She keeps shooting me these looks. Something's up."

Bri leaned closer. "Trouble in paradise."

"Them?" Lydia asked. "Since when? Why hasn't she said anything?"

"Probably hormones," Savannah said. "It took them a while for her to get pregnant. The dust is settling while she's dealing with that. Poor dear. We should go talk to her."

"Or," said Bri, "maybe we should give her some space. If she's grumpy, we don't want her taking it out on us."

"She's not in a bad mood," Savannah said. "I just talked with her a few minutes ago, and she was happy enough."

"Maybe she's mad at me," Lydia said, eying Cara. "I'm not sure why, but I'll ask her after she stops looking at me like that. You guys can talk with her if you want. I'm going to mingle."

"I'm sure everything's fine," Savannah said. She grabbed Bri's hand. "Let's find out what's going on."

Bri stepped back. "You find out what's upsetting Cara. I'm going to mingle with Lyds."

"Sure. Whatever." Savannah shrugged, but looked a little hurt.

"I think I'm getting a headache," Lydia said.

"You and me both," Bri said. "Who do you want to mingle with?"

"Anyone without drama."

Bri hugged her. "Don't worry about Cara. Like Savannah said, it's probably hormones. You haven't done anything to her."

Lydia wandered around the room, not seeing anyone she wanted to talk to. She flinched when she saw Chad. He was sitting with Alyssa, and they were holding hands. They were speaking with another couple, and Chad looked really happy. He turned to Alyssa, and they exchanged a loving look. Lydia's stomach twisted in a knot.

It was the first time she had seen them together.

Bri bumped her arm. Lydia looked over. "Chad?" Bri mouthed. "Chad Mercer?"

Lydia hesitated.

"Oh. My. Gosh." Bri over-emphasized each word. She dragged Lydia to an empty corner. "Your mystery guy was Chad Mercer?"

"It was before everything happened with his family. That was pretty much what ended it, though things were a little muddy for a while even then."

"Chad Mercer."

"Would you stop saying his name?"

"I never would have guessed. He was really planning on leaving?"

"That was the plan." Lydia looked around Bri to sneak another look, and to torture herself. They looked ridiculously happy together.

"But…but he's like the all-American golden boy. They're each other's first loves, right? I remember Alyssa talking about that when Corey and I first moved in."

"Thanks. You don't need to rub it in."

"What kinds of problems were they having?" Bri asked.

"I really don't want to have this conversation."

Bri raised an eyebrow. "You said that you guys talked about everything."

"We did. They couldn't stand to be in the same room as each other. Now, obviously that's changed."

"Oh, honey." Bri gave her another hug. "I can see how much you still love—"

"Mingling. We came here to get to know our neighbors." Lydia stood taller and headed for a group of young married women they rarely talked to. Two of them had bulging bellies, and a third was rocking a baby. "We haven't talked to you guys in so long." Lydia forced a smile. "Congratulations all around."

They spoke about baby showers, and just when Lydia was ready to move to a different group, another young lady ran to the group. She looked excited, and the others asked what was going on.

"We made it into the finals."

The other ladies squealed and hugged her.

Lydia and Bri exchanged a look.

"That sounds exciting," Lydia said, showing her confusion.

"It is. My gorgeous show horse, Flash, just made it into the most prestigious show in the state. This is huge."

"Congratulations," Bri said, showing off her gorgeous smile. She grabbed Lydia's arm, and tugged, obviously wanting to leave the conversation.

Lydia pulled her arm away. "Most prestigious in state? That's incredible."

"I know, right? I'm Dakota, by the way."

"Lydia." She shook hands with Dakota.

"You know about horses?" Bri asked Lydia, raising an eyebrow.

"My mom and I used to watch shows all the time when I was a kid. I was obsessed with horses. My whole room was filled with posters, books, and even horse bedding."

"Really?" asked Dakota.

Lydia nodded. "Tell me all about Flash. How long have you had him?"

Dakota looked down at her hands. "Actually, he's really my brother's. I live vicariously through him. I wish I could live on a big enough piece of land to own my own horses."

"I'd love that, too." Lydia sighed. She hadn't thought about ranch living in years, but it still held a magical appeal.

"Actually, my brother's here. You should meet him." Dakota looked behind Lydia and waved. "Toby!"

Toby came over. He was tall and muscular, with most of his face hidden underneath a cowboy hat. "Ladies." He tipped his hat.

Lydia nearly gasped. He was really hot.

Dakota linked her arm through Lydia's, and smiled at Toby. "This is Lydia, and she wants to know everything about Flash…and she's single."

Bri raised an eyebrow at Lydia.

"Wait. No, I'm not. My—"

"You can't be married," Dakota said. "I live across the street and two doors down. I've seen you hundreds of times, and never once with a guy."

"It's complicated. He travels a lot. He's actually here tonight." Lydia looked around, not seeing him. "Somewhere."

"Complicated?" Dakota asked. She leaned close and whispered in Lydia's ear, "Look at Toby. Isn't he cute? *He's* single."

Lydia looked over at him. "Adorable. He's going to make some lucky girl very happy."

Bri pulled on Lydia. "We've got to find our husbands. Nice meeting you guys."

They barely took two steps when HOA president, Sandra McMillan, clapped her hands. "Time to start the meeting. Let's head over to the chairs."

Lydia looked at Bri. "I didn't think her hair could get any blonder."

"Or bigger," Bri said. "But she manages both."

They sat down, and Dean joined them, next to Lydia. "Having fun?" she asked.

"I remember why I don't like coming to these."

"The food is good, though." Lydia wiped something orange from the corner of his mouth.

He sat taller. "Can't deny that."

"Focus up here, people." Sandra clapped her hands again, this time standing in front. "It's great to see everyone, and lovely to have Dean Harris with us again. Hi, Dean!"

Dean smiled and waved, but Lydia could hear him groaning. Lydia tuned Sandra out, not interested in the association business. Dean leaned over and whispered, "Another reason I hate these things."

Lydia put her hand on his knee. "If you came more often, no one would give you special attention."

He put his hand on top of hers. "And if I didn't come at all, they wouldn't ever have occasion to put me on the spot."

"But they would still ask about you. They always do—every month."

Bri nudged Lydia. "Shh. Some of us are trying to listen."

Lydia rolled her eyes. She knew Bri wasn't paying any more attention to Sandra than Lydia was. Lydia looked around and noticed Chad and Alyssa sitting a couple rows in front of them. They stole a kiss and Lydia felt a lump form in her throat, her hand sandwiched between Dean's knee and hand.

She tried to take her attention away from the Mercers but she couldn't stop looking. Chad whispered into Alyssa's ear every so often. He wrapped his arm around her. Then he played with her hair. She looked over at him and smiled.

Bri leaned over and whispered in Lydia's ear, "Stop torturing yourself."

"Am I being that obvious?"

"Now that I know, yes."

Lydia looked up at Sandra.

She was discussing the color someone wanted to paint their house. It wasn't a pre-approved color so they had to vote. "All who agree on shade number 325 Wenge, raise your hands."

Lydia raised her hand, not caring either way. As long as it wasn't something ridiculous like violet or magenta, she really didn't care. The meeting dragged on. Sandra appeared to love every minute of it, but Lydia was all too aware of Dean squirming next to her. Normally, he would yell at her about it when they got home—why had she dragged him there? But with any luck, his good mood would continue.

Finally, an hour later, the meeting ended. Dean practically dragged her to the door. "I can't take another minute of this. You still like that Italian place by the mall?"

"You mean Gianotti's? I love it."

"Let's go. They make strong drinks, and I need a couple."

"Okay." Lydia couldn't help smiling. It was almost like the old Dean, the one she had married, was back. She would take him as long as he would stay around. Maybe he would even help her to forget about Chad. Going to the meeting had only made that worse.

It felt so good to have him back. The way he kept looking at Lydia made her feel like a newlywed again. Sneaking away from the meeting before it ended reminded her of their early days together, when they were carefree and didn't have a worry in the world except for spending time together.

She thought back to the clippings. It was ridiculous of her to jump to the conclusion that he was a murderer. A killer, of all things.

He smiled at her as they made their way to the door. Butterflies danced in her stomach. There was no way he had killed anyone. If anything, he was investigating those murders and didn't want anyone to know. Dean's job was so secretive, it was possible that he had to lead a double life in order to solve the cases.

They made their way back to their house and then got into Dean's car.

"I don't even think I've been in here before," Lydia said. He had shown up with it one day, and since he barely ever spoke to her, they had no reason to go anywhere in it.

"Really? Not once?"

"Nope." She sniffed. "It still has the new car smell."

"Once that's gone, it's time for a new car."

They made small talk on the way to the restaurant. Once there, he ordered one drink after another and talked even more, telling Lydia about the exciting changes taking place at his work. It was the first she had heard anything about any of it, but she smiled and encouraged him to keep talking. As he went on, and she listened, she couldn't help wondering what was going on.

His sudden attention had to have something to do with the newspaper, which made it feel more like he was guilty. That meant that he was just trying to keep her on his good side...and that she was sitting across from a murderer. Not just a one-timer, either. It had been going on for at least a couple years.

Lydia sighed. She didn't know what to think. Was the new—old—Dean a good thing or a bad thing?

Dean laughed loudly as he finished up some story about a friend from work. Lydia smiled and said something to sound engaged. She watched him, conflicted. On one hand, she saw the man she had fallen in love with so long ago. It felt like decades, but they hadn't reached their seven-year itch yet. On the other hand, she also saw the man who had refused to touch her for so long. But given Lydia's recent findings, that was probably a good thing.

She didn't want to be involved with a serial killer, but getting away was the tricky part. If she initiated a divorce, she risked his wrath. The last thing she wanted was to end up on a clipping under their floorboards. If she left before saying anything, she would always have to look over her shoulder. One thing she had learned from her years of marriage....

No one crossed Dean Harris.

Discussion

CARA SAT DOWN on the couch next to Ethan. He glanced her way, not taking his attention off the show and then scooted over away from her.

"Why do you find me so repulsive?" asked Cara, frowning.

Ethan picked up the remote from the cushion and turned the TV off. "Do you think I'm stupid, Cara?"

Cara's heart dropped into her stomach. "What do you mean, hon?" She forced a smile.

He narrowed his eyes. "You never told me the results of our fertility testing."

She stared at him. He couldn't know. He just couldn't.

Ethan continued, "I've been waiting for you to come clean."

Cara's heart pounded so loud it sounded like it was in her ears.

"You're planning on pretending we can be a happy family—with someone else's baby."

"I…I…what are you talking about?"

"You're going to play dumb, even now?" Ethan's face grew red and his spit landed on her face.

"What are you talking about?" Cara snapped. "I'm not playing."

He laughed.

"You know what I mean." She folded her arms.

"Whose baby is it?" Ethan narrowed his eyes.

"Ethan, it's yours…ours. We're going to be a family."

"I'm not an idiot, Cara."

"I never said you were."

"Then have enough respect for me to tell the truth." He stepped closer, furrowing his eyebrows.

"We're a family. You, me, and the baby."

"Oh, stop. We both *know* someone else fathered the baby. I have proof."

"You…you…can't…how?" Cara sputtered.

Ethan's eyebrows came together. "I've left the chatty Cara speechless? That's a first." He shook his head. "I knew the fertility results were due, so I called the clinic from work. Imagine my surprise to find out that you'd known for weeks. I actually gave you the benefit of the doubt. I thought you were in so much pain that you couldn't bring yourself to say it."

"I was," Cara whispered.

"Right." Ethan sat up straight. "That's why a week later you came to me with your pregnancy results. I have zero chance of having a child naturally." His voice cracked. "None, Cara!"

She stared at him.

"But you knew that already—you knew before I did. If you had your way, I still wouldn't know, would I?"

"Ethan, I—"

"Did you know they have procedures that could've helped us have kids, even though my sperm count is so low?" His eyes shone with tears. "You didn't have to jump in bed with the first guy you saw—or were you already seeing him?"

"No. It's not like that, Ethan. I've always been true to you."

He stared at her bulging belly and laughed. "Right. I can see that. Some other man's baby is in you."

"I wasn't trying to cheat on you."

"How did it happen?" Ethan's lips formed a straight line and he stared into her eyes.

Cara took a deep breath. "I didn't mean for it to happen. When I found out, you were at work. I ran to talk to one of my friends." Cara looked away, considering her words carefully. Then she decided just to spit it out. "She wasn't home, but her husband was…and when it was over, I couldn't believe what I'd just done."

"Right."

"It's true."

"Oh?" he asked. "Your clothes just happened to come off, and he accidentally knocked you up?"

"I didn't mean for it to happen."

"Yet you let it happen, anyway. Who is the father?"

Cara looked away, tears blurring her vision.

"Who is it?" shouted Ethan.

"Does it matter? We can still be a family. Think of it as an adoption, only without the paperwork."

"Have you lost your mind?"

"Of course not. We're married, and legally, the child is yours."

"Who's the father?" Ethan demanded.

"You are."

"Cara, you're the most annoying, lying sack of—"

"It's Dean."

Ethan swore. "Dean? Your *best friend's* husband? Have you told Lydia?"

Cara blinked tears onto her face and then shook her head.

"Does Dean know it's his? Or was it a one-time thing, and you've been lying to everyone involved?"

"He knows."

"Really?" Ethan grabbed some of his hair and pulled it tight into his fist. "So his friendliness at the meeting was a lie. He knew he'd betrayed our friendship, and he acted like nothing was wrong. Does he plan on raising it?"

"No." More tears fell.

Ethan punched the arm of the couch. "You really thought this would work? You lying about the father?"

"I thought it could work. You'll be a great father."

He stared at her, and Cara could feel the fury. She had never seen him so upset before. "Are you still seeing him?"

Cara couldn't find the words. They were stuck in her throat.

"Answer me!"

Cara jumped. "The man who's only home a few days a month?"

Ethan's nostrils flared. "That's not an answer to my question. Have you seen him since that one time?"

"Obviously when I told him about the baby."

"You slept with him then, too?" Ethan exclaimed.

"That's not what I meant."

"It's what I meant. Have you slept with him since the night of conception? Answer me."

Cara looked down at her freshly manicured nails. More tears escaped as she nodded.

"Look at me and answer!"

A large lump in Cara's throat nearly choked her. She looked at Ethan. "Yes. It happened again."

Ethan shook his head, his face reddening. "You know, if it was just that one time...I could see trying to make it work. Maybe. But you've been back with him? How dare you tell me it was a mistake when you've been with him since then?"

"Because you're disgusted by me!" she shouted.

He grabbed her arm. "That's where you're mistaken. I've been disgusted by knowing you're carrying another man's baby. I was hoping you'd talk to me about it, but instead you've been acting like nothing's wrong. We're through, Cara."

"What? No. You can't do this."

"I can't do this?" he yelled, standing. "And why not, exactly? I work sixty-plus hours a week so you can stay home and pamper yourself. You play with the other spoiled housewives all day while I work myself to the bone. Believe it or not, I've always been fine with that. I take my role as provider seriously, but when you step out on me like that—repeatedly—I won't stand for it. You need to find someplace else to live."

"What?" Cara felt cold and began shivering. "You can't do this to me. Where will I go?"

"You should have thought about that before you started a relationship with your best friend's husband. Maybe Lydia will let you stay at her place. Should I call her?"

Cara jumped up. "You wouldn't."

"No. You're right. I'll leave that to you. You'd better start packing. I need to contact my attorney."

"But you—"

"Don't worry. You'll be more than fairly compensated. I don't want a huge court battle. I'll give you more than you ever would be granted by a court so long as you don't hire your own attorney and fight me. Then I won't give you a thing more than I'm required to."

Cara stared at him, the weight of everything nearly crushing her.

"Despite all this, Cara, I still love you. I really wanted you to say that it was a one-time thing and that you regretted it with your whole heart. That's what I hoped you would say...and I hoped you would say it without me asking." He walked away.

"When are you kicking me out?"

Ethan turned around. "I'm not cruel. You can stay in one of the guest rooms for tonight at least, but you need to think seriously about where you're going after this." He turned around and left the room. Cara could hear him dialing his cell phone.

She sat on the couch and sobbed into her hands. Why had she been so stupid to think she could pull it off? Ethan was right. She had betrayed the ones she loved most. Cara had convinced herself that Lydia wouldn't care—and maybe she wouldn't, but if Cara had been so sure, why had she gone out of her way to keep it hidden from her? Because it would hurt Lydia...or because Cara was afraid one of her best friends would hate her?

They had grown so close when Lydia had been seeing her mystery man. Cara knew it was Chad Mercer. She had figured it out just watching Lydia at the HOA meetings. Though she tried to be discreet, Lydia watched him like a lost puppy. Cara could see it in her eyes: Chad was the one who had Lydia's heart.

Her lips quivered. Looking at him, she realized how much she loved him and didn't want to lose him. She stood up. "Ethan, I was stupid. I never should've let it happen, not even once. No matter how much I was upset about us not being able to have a baby. Please, can we work this out?"

"How many times, Cara?" Ethan asked.

Cara looked away, unable to speak.

"You can't even tell me?"

"It's not like I kept count," she whispered.

"So many times you can't even remember?" He punched a wall.

"I thought you hated me. I promise never to see him again. Please. Let's work this out."

Sadness covered his face, replacing the look of rage. "I wish I could say yes, but I can't trust you. Without trust, what are we left with?"

"I can go into counseling. I can change." Cara ran over to him and clung to him. "I'll do anything, Ethan. I was stupid. Do you hear me? Stupid. I was wrong. I'll do whatever I can to make it up to you. No matter what you say, I'll do it. I don't care how humiliating it is. I'll publicly apologize. Whatever you want."

He kissed the top of her head. "Begging isn't pretty, Cara. It doesn't suit you."

She looked into his eyes. "I don't care. I can't lose you."

"You should have thought about that all those times you slept with Dean."

"I'll cut it off with him. I promise to never speak to him, or even look at him ever again. You have my word."

"Cut it off? It's serious enough for you to use that phrase?"

"No. That's not what I meant. I just—"

"Cara, stop while you're ahead."

"Ahead? Ahead of what?" She looked around in desperation, trying to find something to say to convince him to give it another chance.

"I'm leaving your infidelity out of the divorce proceedings. Remember the prenuptial agreement my parents insisted we sign?"

A horrible sound escaped Cara's throat. She'd forgotten all about the prenup. It felt as though the world was going to crush her.

"How are you going to explain…?" She looked down at her stomach.

"Simple. I won't mention it. I know you're not going to come after me for any kind of support. A simple blood test would prevent me from any responsibility. That's only if my medical records don't—"

"Okay. Please stop. I get it."

"You really should get packing. You've got twenty-four hours to figure something out."

Cara stepped back, defeated. "I'm basically walking away with my clothes and jewelry, and that's it?"

"I told you I'm going to give you more than the courts would. I'll put your car in your name, but you'll be responsible for the payments now." He pointed to the kitchen table. "Your grandparents gave us the kitchen set. You can take it. That lamp by the TV, I know how much you love it. It's yours."

"But your mom picked it out for us."

Ethan looked into her eyes and took her hand. His eyes shone with tears. "As heartbroken as I am, I still want you to be happy. The last thing I could wish on you would be anything ill. I just can't be married to you any longer. I'm sorry, Cara. I really hoped you'd come to me and admit your one-time mistake so we could work through this."

"But we can make this work. I'll stop seeing Dean—I mean, I won't ever look at him again. You know what I mean. Like I said, I'll do anything you want."

"I said I don't want you to beg." He wiped tears away from his eyes. "This kills me, Cara. I really wanted to grow old with you. But I can't ever move past this. Not an intentional affair."

Cara's eyes widened. "It wasn't an affair, Ethan. It was a mistake."

He shook he his head, his entire body shaking. "Not when it happened that many times and you use phrases like 'cut it off.' I wish this could be repaired."

"It can't."

He shook his head and then cleared his throat. "You need to move out, Cara."

"Aren't you afraid of what people will think? You kicking your pregnant wife out?"

He raised an eyebrow. "I'm sure you won't allow anyone to think anything like that."

Cara shook her head. "No."

"You'd better get packing. I'll hire someone for the bigger stuff. You'll need help unloading it wherever you go."

"How can I find someplace in just a day?"

"You're resourceful. I'm sure you can do it." He walked away, dialing his phone again.

"Wait!"

He turned around and looked at her.

"How am I going to pay for a place to live? No one is going to hire me. Not after they take one look at me."

"I'll take care of your first month. Give you a chance to get on your feet. Or you can always move in with your mom. She always says she never sees you enough."

"I'd rather live in an apartment."

"Suit yourself." He held up his phone, still looking deflated, and showed her the time. "Moving closer to twenty-three hours."

Cara looked around. The house felt like it was suffocating her. It was her home—she had thought she would grow old there. Now she had less than a day to figure out where she was going to move. She would never again see the inside of the walls. She looked around. Her touch was everywhere. Ethan didn't care about decorating. She had picked out nearly everything in sight, but only a small percentage of it would be hers. And if she tried to fight him, even less would be.

Countdown

SWEAT BROKE OUT on Cara's forehead. It was past two in the morning, but she didn't know by how much. The last time she'd looked at the clock it was just after, but that felt like hours ago. She slid another book into the box. Another piece of her life packed away.

Her lower back ached, but there was no time to worry about that. Anything left in the house after the twenty-four hour mark would stay. Why had she slept with Dean when she had signed a prenuptial agreement? Probably because she had forgotten all about it. Ethan had never once mentioned it since they signed it, and even then he had been so nonchalant about it.

Cara was a true rags-to-riches story, and that was why his parents—mostly his mother—had insisted on the agreement. If she had come from a world of private schools and golf lessons, that wretched woman probably wouldn't have said a word about it. But because she hadn't come from wealth, and because that shrew had nagged her son into a prenup, Cara now had no leg to stand on.

That was one thing she recalled from the paperwork. If she slept with anyone else, she would lose everything gained from marriage, only walking away with what she had brought in. Ethan was being much kinder than he needed to be. Cara knew that much. She also knew he had probably spoken the truth—if she had been with Dean only the first time, he would have given it a chance.

A pain shot through her belly, so she sat down on the nearest chair. She was pushing herself too far, but what other choice did she have? She wasn't going to get an extra minute to pack, and she still had no idea where she was going. A small moving truck was scheduled to arrive, but there was no destination.

Her stomach squeezed. Maybe she needed a little sleep. The last thing she needed was to send herself into premature labor. It was way too early, and she would lose the baby for sure. That little person nestled beneath her ribs was all she had left in the world. A tear slid down her face, and she wiped it away.

Cara left the box where it was and headed for the nearest guest room. She needed to rest. She set the alarm on her cell phone as she walked. The pains in her stomach and the ache in her back continued, but she thought they were easing up. It was hard to tell.

Maybe, just maybe, Ethan would give Cara some more time if she was having pregnancy-related problems. He was mad, but not cruel.

She slid into the bed, surprised at how comfortable it was. They hadn't put much thought into the guest furniture, or at least she hadn't. Ethan might have. Cara was realizing just how thoughtful he really was. That was something she hadn't paid attention to in a long time.

Cara found a semi-comfortable position and closed her eyes. Her mind raced, not allowing her tired body to sleep. She put her hands on her stomach and tried not to think about anything.

Would she still be able to be friends with Bri, Savannah, and Lydia? With Lydia, that would depend on a lot of things. She might be furious at Cara. Lydia had wanted to have a baby with Dean so badly, but then she fell in love with Chad, so it was possible she didn't care about Dean anymore. Cara had a hard time believing their lovebird show at the HOA meeting.

Lydia had been acting strange, but then why would she have been holding Dean's hand at the meeting?

Cara had had mixed feelings about seeing them together. At first she'd been upset, but then she thought it would be good for her friend, even if it meant Dean had to cut things off with her.

Now Cara didn't know what she wanted from Dean. Did she want to see if he would raise the baby with her? If she did that, she could kiss her friendship with Lydia goodbye. Even if Lydia didn't care about Dean, it would just be too awkward. Bri might also be mad at her. She was close to Lydia and wasn't happy about Dean being the dad, but she couldn't say anything due to Cara knowing her secret.

Cara pulled the pillow over her head. Why couldn't she stop thinking? Her stomach felt better, so the rest was what she needed. But she was wasting time if she couldn't sleep.

Worry about her friends, and even Dean, was useless. She didn't know where she was going to bed the next night. The last place Cara wanted to go was to her mom's, but the more she thought about it, the better it probably was. She wasn't going to tell any of her friends about the split up.

What would they think of her going back to the poor part of town? They probably didn't even know what part of town Cara was from. It wasn't like she ever made a point to talk about it. Quite the opposite, in fact. Cara went out of her way to dress up the truth so no one would know that she had grown up poor. Cara made fun of the *trailer trash,* but in reality, those were her people—at least they used to be. Now they might be again.

She didn't even want to take her *stuff* to the trailer, much less her baby. Her mom had an unemployed, drunk bum of a boyfriend living with her, and Cara didn't trust him. No, going there would be a bad idea. Like she had told Ethan, she'd rather live in an apartment. But that would require getting a job, and who would hire her? She was at the point where she couldn't hide her pregnancy no matter what she wore. Not that she was even qualified for anything, having only barely graduated from college.

Cara rolled over and focused on the black behind her eyes. "Just sleep," she whispered. Ethan had offered to help her get on her feet for a month. She didn't need to figure everything out right then. When she woke up, she could look for an apartment. Then after she got settled in, she could figure out what she would do for a job.

Dean might even have some ideas. If he knew Cara was suddenly on her own, he would be willing to help her out. She sat up. That was it. Dean had a condo somewhere not too far away. She was the mother of his child—surely he would let her stay there. Then she could save the money Ethan gave her and let Dean take care of her.

She could be sweet and take care of him and keep the condo shining.

Then he would see how great it would be for the two of them to be together. He could get a second house and they could live happily together when he was avoiding Lydia. Or maybe he would leave her altogether.

That was it. It would work out perfectly. Cara slid under the covers, finally feeling sleepy. Maybe everything was going to work out just like it should. She would have a family with her baby's actual dad. It was perfect. She only had to get a hold of Dean to find out where his condo was. By dinnertime, she could be sipping iced tea by a pool.

Her eyelids, now heavy, closed. Cara slipped into a peaceful sleep knowing that everything would somehow work out. Even if she lost her best friend. Besides, she had known that was a possibility from the moment she kissed Dean that fateful night.

The alarm on her cell woke Cara up around seven. She was surprised at how rested she felt after only about four hours of sleep. She stretched, enjoying the feeling that had settled into her body as she slept.

As Cara turned off the alarm, she noticed a missed text. It was from an unknown number: *The coffee is ground.*

Cara smiled and held the phone close. It was Dean's secret code. He was settled in and had a number she could call. When he traveled, he always bought a throwaway phone. Once it was activated, he texted her something about caffeine, and she could call or text at that number until he left. It was the perfect solution to make sure neither of their spouses ever figured out what was going on.

She always kept her phone password protected, but at least with the changing numbers, neither Ethan nor Lydia would never know about their conversations if they checked the phone records.

Ethan appeared in the doorway. "I'm going into the office, but I'll be back before the truck gets here. Make sure you know where you're going by then. Otherwise, I'll give them your mom's address."

Cara's stomach twisted in knots. "No. I'll find an apartment."

He nodded and then disappeared.

She looked at the time. Considering all she had to do, she needed to get back to packing. She would have to skip a shower today, as much as she hated the thought of it.

Cara found Dean's latest text and hit reply. *I love coffee grounds.* She had to send a single message in response to his to let him know that she got it, and it also confirmed that no one else knew what was going on.

Did you sleep well?

No. We need to talk. Are you available now?

She sat and waited for two long minutes. Sometimes he was in a meeting or otherwise busy with work. She knew better than to take it personally.

Can you text me the details? I'm tied up at the moment.

How could she text all of that to him? Cara took a deep breath and thought about how to sum everything up as concisely as possible. *Ethan knows.*

No response. Cara's heart sped up, but she knew Dean would have to process the shock.

Everything?

Pretty much. Do you have room in your condo for me?

Cara waited a full five minutes. Then she typed a new message. *I can always get an apartment. It's no biggie.* Her finger hovered over the send button. She held her breath, hoping she hadn't overstepped her bounds and upset him. She knew from Lydia's stories that Dean could go crazy when he lost his temper.

I have a better idea.

Cara let out her breath and deleted her message. *What's that?*

I've been looking at a couple of foreclosures by the lake. I'll have my real estate attorney see if they're still available and have him fax me the papers.

Could I go there tonight?

I'll see what I can do. Talk later. Xoxo

Xoxo

Cara breathed another sigh of relief. Not only was he taking it well, but he was getting a house on the lake for the two of them.

Planning

LYDIA WOKE UP to an empty bed. Dean was gone, but a single rose rested in his spot. She picked it up and smelled it. The scent was strong and sweet, lingering even after she put it back where she'd found it.

When they had returned home after dinner, Dean had kissed her neck again and they had their second marital encounter for the day... and the last three or four years. Lydia wasn't sure. She used to keep track of how long it had been since he started ignoring her, but after falling in love with Chad, she had not only stopped but forgotten the dates.

Lydia yawned and stretched. She tried to remember how long he would be gone this time. She wasn't sure he had even told her. That meant she would have to check the calendar. She got the chills and shivered just thinking about it.

Dean was being nice, but one thing she had learned was that meant nothing. He knew how to put on a show and make people think what he wanted them to. He was slick, and he knew it. That was how he had tricked her into marrying him. He wasn't the man he pretended to be.

The man from the previous day, that was who he pretended to be to get her to marry him. He had continued his charade until just past their first anniversary, giving her the first year of her dreams. The stage had been set. Lydia thought she had the perfect life—doting husband, beautiful house, and plenty of nice things.

Their relationship had turned sour quickly, surprising her. Lydia had spent hours trying to figure out what had gone wrong. What had been the real cause of their problems? The big thing was not being able to have a baby, but the truth was that when he agreed to travel for work—without asking her what she thought—that was when things changed, but on a smaller scale.

Lydia would never forget the day he told her about the traveling. The day she first caught a glimpse of his true colors. He had taken her to a restaurant, most likely to keep her from freaking out. They were at a busy seafood place, and the meal had just arrived. The buzz of the conversation all around made Lydia think she had heard him wrong.

"What did you say?" she asked. "It sounded like you said you agreed to take a traveling position."

Dean nodded. "I did. It's the promotion of my dreams."

She would have felt less hurt if he had slapped her across the face. "Why have I never heard anything about it?" She shook, but tried to hide it.

"I never thought it was a possibility. Weston Smith who has had the position for years announced that he wanted to settle in one place. Several other guys want this position, but I'm the highest seniority. If I want it, it's mine. No one higher up the chain wants it."

Lydia put her fork down, unable to eat anymore. "But still, why wouldn't you have said anything to me?"

"I told you. I didn't think it would ever happen. I want to go to the moon, too, but what's the point in discussing that? It's not going to happen."

"Is there anything else you're not telling me? Something that doesn't seem important, but could be if it actually happened?"

He smiled, practically looking smug. "With this position comes a raise. A huge one, Lyds. You're going to love the figures. My salary is going to more than double."

Lydia froze, holding his eye contact.

"It's true. We can get a house in that neighborhood you always drool over. I've already taken a peek, and there are two houses for sale right now. You could have your pick."

Dean always knew what to say to get what he wanted. He was right, she had been wanting to move into that area for as long as she could remember. Lydia had even offered to get a job so they could move in there, but Dean would have nothing to do with his wife working. It was a bragging point that she didn't have to.

It didn't matter what she wanted, just how things appeared.

"When do you start?" she asked.

"Next week. While I'm away, why don't you tour the available homes, and decide what you like best?" He smiled, melting her. He was giving her what she wanted, and he loved every minute of it.

Lydia knew what he was doing, but was too excited about the house. Moving into that neighborhood was something she had wanted so badly that she could feel it. Dean was giving it to her to soften the blow about his new job, and it worked exactly as he had planned.

The next time Lydia complained about him traveling, he took her car shopping. He thought he could buy her off, and for a little while, it worked. Until he ran out of things she wanted. Lydia had many things that made her friends green with envy. Expensive shoes and purses, imported furniture, and so much more.

Dean had been able to keep her happy—distracted was more accurate—for a while, until they started trying to have a baby. Once he couldn't give her what she wanted most, things turned sour fast.

Lydia sat up in bed, not wanting to think about it anymore. She picked up the rose and put it in a vase in the bathroom. Was a rose now supposed to keep her happy? If she couldn't come up with a good plan before he came back, she would have to pretend. At least she was good at that.

She went downstairs and checked his calendar. He was supposed to be gone exactly one week. Lydia wasn't sure that was enough time to get everything in order. A divorce would likely be time-consuming. She had seen several friends go through those, and there was always a huge hang-up every time.

Lydia made some organic oatmeal and thought about her chances. She didn't work, so really, everything they had was his. The house and the cars were in his name. He had said they needed to be, because he was the one with the income. She had credit cards, but he was the primary on all their accounts, and he could revoke her access at any time.

The longer she thought about it, the more discouraged she became. Lawyers would probably send her packing with just the clothes on her back. She had come in with nothing, she had gained nothing, and she would leave with exactly that. Unless she could prove his guilt or find a way to convince him to let her have more.

He wouldn't give her anything out of the kindness of his heart. If she confronted him with what little she knew, there would be nothing stopping him from killing her, too. Dean would know she had that information and could use it against him anytime. Even if that were a possibility, then she would be guilty of not turning in a killer.

She let out a long, frustrated breath. There had to be another option. Maybe she could set aside some cash, get away from him, and then send in an anonymous tip. Then she wouldn't be in the position to have to prove anything. The cops would be responsible for comparing his travels to the crimes committed.

Dean would probably know who ratted him out, even if she was gone. Lydia would have to make sure she was somewhere far away that he would never think to look. Going to her family was out, because that would be the first place he looked for her. What if he hurt them, trying to find her?

He wouldn't do that if the police were watching him. Once they knew he was a suspect in a string of killings, he would have to be on his best behavior. Lydia didn't have the luxury of worrying about her family. She needed to take care of herself. No matter what happened, Dean would know that she knew, or at least suspected something.

Did he already think she knew? Could he be planning her demise on the plane right then? Lydia's pulse pounded in her ears. There was only one thing she couldn't do—nothing. She had to do something, and the sooner the better. His recent kindness was nothing more than a show.

He knew he had screwed up big time, dropping the paper for her to find it. Whether he actually thought she knew anything, that was anyone's guess. And it wasn't something Lydia was going to wait around to find out about.

Lydia stayed in the chair just thinking. The rest of her breakfast went cold and she ignored several calls from Bri. She thought about all of her options, and eventually decided it was best to play detective.

What she really needed was proof. If she could prove to the cops that he was dangerous and killing people, they would have no choice but to lock him up. Then she wouldn't have to move or anything. She might have to get a real job, but that wouldn't be so bad. She had wanted to work when they first got married.

Working would be far better than living in fear, which is what would end up happening if she waited and did nothing. So far, he obviously hadn't killed her. She didn't know why, but she was going to use that to her advantage. If she needed to take a few months to piece everything together, then she would just pretend to be the happy housewife when he was home.

Her phone rang again, and it was Bri again. She threw it across to the living room where it bounced on the carpet several times. Lydia wasn't going to see some movie when she had real problems to figure out.

She grabbed a glass of wine and went onto the porch to sit in the sun. There was a week until Dean came back. That would give her some time, but not enough to get done everything she needed. If only he was going to be gone for two to three weeks like he often was. Why was he suddenly coming home more frequently—right after she had found his stuff?

Lydia didn't want to live on the run or in hiding. That was for the movies. No, she was a smart and capable woman. She would find enough proof to get him arrested, and then let the authorities do the rest.

Could she do that in a week? Maybe if he had left enough damning evidence in the house, but even if he had, how would she find it? It had been an accident that she even found the box in the floorboards. Their house was close to four thousand square feet if you counted the garage.

Lydia had her work cut out for her.

Preparing

LYDIA WIPED SWEAT from her forehead as she walked out of Dean's office. He'd been smart enough not to leave any incriminating evidence in the most obvious of places. That was where he spent most of his waking hours when he was home. There wasn't anything anywhere, not even a loose piece of carpet. Lydia had even searched every file on his computer, but chances were anything useful would be on his laptop, which always went with him.

She grabbed a glass of water and drank it down in a couple of gulps. Lydia filled the glass again, trying to decide where to look next. Her stomach rumbled, and she looked at the time. It was getting close to dinnertime. How had that happened? It must have taken her longer than she thought to go through the office. It certainly hadn't felt that long.

Her phone rang. She went over to where it had landed earlier. It was Bri, and it looked like she had missed eight calls.

"Hi, Bri."

"So your phone *does* work."

"Sorry. I was…cleaning and lost track of time."

"Cleaning?" Bri didn't sound convinced.

"Sure. Don't you ever get into a streak where you just feel like you have to clean?"

"Yeah, but that usually involves making room so I can go shopping. You planning a trip to the mall?" Bri sounded hopeful.

"I just want to go through some stuff."

"So, I don't need to worry about you?"

That was a loaded question. "Nah. I'm fine."

"How's Dean?"

"I wouldn't know. He doesn't usually call when he's traveling. But he did leave a flower when he left this morning."

"Aww. That's so sweet. What changed?"

"I'm not really sure. Maybe he had a row with his girlfriend."

"So you don't think he's changed?"

"Not unless he quit traveling and spent all his time doting on me."

"We missed you today."

"Was the movie good?"

Bri paused. "We didn't see it. The girls and I just talked at the restaurant. Want to catch it tomorrow?"

Lydia held in a groan. "Maybe. Let me see how much cleaning I can get done tonight. I'm on a roll, and I don't want to stop if I can help it."

"Want some help?"

"No," Lydia said too fast. "I mean, you wouldn't have any fun. You hate to clean."

"You know me too well. But if you get bored or just want to talk, give me a call."

"Will do. Thanks for checking on me, Bri."

"What are friends for?"

The call ended, and Lydia let out a sigh of relief. She wasn't going to be able to keep a secret from Bri for long, but for the time being Lydia wasn't going to breathe a word of her suspicions to anyone.

Her stomach growled again. "I better eat before deciding what to go through next."

Lydia looked in the fridge and saw leftovers from the night before. It would have to do, because she was in no mood for cooking. She slopped some food onto a plate and stuck it in the microwave.

She paused, watching it rotate inside. What if Dean really was killing people? If he suspected her snooping, would he try to poison her food? Her stomach twisted in knots.

No. He was being so sweet. She had no reason to doubt his intentions toward her.

After eating, she went up to the bedroom and went through Dean's drawers. She found nothing unusual, but that wasn't surprising, especially after finding his office clean. She would have to get more creative than going through his socks.

She went back into the closet. Could there have been more clues in there? Or had he hidden more things around the house in sneaky places like that? Maybe she could find another clue in his papers.

Lydia pulled her hair behind her shoulder and then moved the safe back. She pulled the carpet back, and then lifted the floorboards. The little space was empty.

Her blood ran cold as she stared at the empty area. He had moved his box of clippings? She reached down and felt around, half-expecting a mousetrap to snap onto her fingers. But there was nothing—nothing—in the little space.

Did Dean know she had found his stuff or did he make a habit of moving things around?

Maybe she never should have given him back the paper he dropped. She should have let him wonder, not to mention sweat, about what had happened to it.

Lydia replaced everything and then leaned against the wall. At least she had taken pictures of everything. It would be harder to read the pictures from her phone, but it was better than nothing.

She opened the gallery of photos on the screen, but her back tingled. She looked around, feeling as though she was being watched. Dean wasn't around, but had he set up a hidden camera?

No. She was just imagining things. Her back continued tingling, but it didn't matter. If he was recording her, he already had her discovering the empty cubby under the floor. Surely a camera wouldn't be able to pick up what she was looking at on her phone.

The feelings wouldn't go away, so she got up from the bed and went into the rarely-used guest room. It could just as easily be bugged, but she didn't feel imaginary stares in there.

Lydia sat at the desk and found the picture of the first newspaper clipping. She enlarged the image and then scanned it for clues, not coming up with anything. She moved onto the rest, looking for similarities between them, or at least something else to jump out at her.

Nothing did.

The only thing that any of them had in common was the fact that they could have possibly been killed by the same person. But no one else would be able to put that together, because no one else had found them all hidden together.

Dean was actually pretty brilliant, assuming it was him. Someone would have to know his traveling schedule to figure it out, to put everything together. If the police were searching for similar cases, they would be on the lookout for victims in similar areas. These women were all over the place, spread throughout the country with one in Canada.

What she needed to do was to get online and see what more had been found. Were there any new clues? There had to be. The investigations couldn't all couldn't be stalled. Did she dare search on her laptop, or would she be better off going to the library? Would they want her to log in with her library card? That would send more red flags than anything else. Lydia wanted to be even more careful than Dean.

If he figured out she was onto him… no, she wasn't going to let that happen. Not before she took it to the authorities. Now she had even less proof since he had taken the box.

There had to be a way to look into all of this without it leading back to her. She would almost need a new identity. Or at least an online one. She could purchase a cheap laptop with cash, open up a fake email account, and store everything there. She would also have to go somewhere with free wi-fi and never let the computer connect to the home internet.

It was a lot of trouble, but if she was living with a serial killer, she had every right to know. No matter what crazy hoops she had to jump through.

Lydia turned her phone off and leaned back in the chair. Part of her wanted to call one of her friends and tell them everything. She had always been close with Bri. That was why she wouldn't leave Lydia alone—she had to know something was wrong. Cara and she had been close for a while, but then around the time Cara got pregnant, she also distanced herself from Lydia. Most likely because Cara knew how much it hurt her that she couldn't have a baby. Savannah and Lydia had often shared secrets, too.

She trusted all of them, but she couldn't lay that on them, at least not until she knew more. Lydia needed to protect the ones she loved. For now, the less they knew, the better.

Lydia got up, went to her car, and drove to the bank. She went to a branch that she rarely went to so no one would remember her. She would just be another customer. Everyone knew her from the one inside her grocery store. Lydia could just imagine one of the cute tellers innocently telling Dean she saw his wife come in and take out cash.

Then Lydia would raise his suspicions and possibly be next on his list…if she wasn't already. She sat in the parking lot pretending to fix her makeup, but she was actually pretending to look natural. If she walked in looking as nervous as she felt, everyone would think she was going to rob the place.

She took a few deep breaths and reminded herself that she wasn't the one who had done anything wrong, and in fact, she still wasn't doing anything wrong. Why hadn't she set any money aside for herself in a different bank? It wouldn't have taken much, especially with her magazine job. If she had just taken five or ten percent of that each month, she would have had a nice stash for herself. Now it would be harder to sneak money from her shared account.

Lydia made a mental note to set up her own bank account somewhere else and have part of her earnings go there. Then she grabbed her purse and walked into the bank. All of the lines were full, and several people stood waiting. Perfect. Everyone was too busy to notice her.

Everyone except the little kid in front of her. The boy stood only a foot away from his mom, a big flop of blonde hair getting into his eyes. He bounced from one foot to the other, staring at Lydia.

She looked away but could still see him watching her out of the corner of her eye. He moved closer to her, and Lydia looked down, making eye contact. The boy jumped to his mom and wrapped himself around her leg, burying his face into her floral pencil skirt.

Lydia managed to get to the counter without anyone else taking any special note of her.

The teller smiled, showing lipstick on her teeth. "What can I do for you today?"

She wanted to say, *Wipe your teeth.* Instead, she slid the withdrawal slip and her ATM card on the counter. "Just a withdrawal."

"Sure, no problem." She entered everything into the computer while Lydia pretended to be bored. "Here you go. Have a nice day." She handed Lydia the cash and her card.

Lydia slid it into her purse. "You, too." She went back to her car and headed for Costco. It was the cheapest place she knew of to buy a computer. She had seen some laptops for just a couple hundred dollars last time she'd been in. She had been looking for a small TV to put on the wall in the kitchen, but somehow ended up checking out computers.

After arriving at Costco, she found herself looking at the same row of computers and laptops she had seen before. This time, the cheapest one was gone, but there was one only about fifty dollars more. She purchased it, hoping that Dean didn't have a way to find out what had been purchased since she had to use their membership card. With any luck, he was too busy with his own work to keep tabs on her like that.

Questioning

"**L**YDS STILL ISN'T answering," Bri said. "I hope she's okay." She looked at her phone as if it could give her the answers, and then she glanced around the restaurant, hoping to see Lydia walking toward them.

"We should go to the movie without her," Cara said. "Obviously, she's not interested in what you have to say."

"Touchy much?" Bri asked.

"She's stonewalling you, Bri. She's fine—just doesn't want to talk to you."

"You saw her and Dean at the meeting." Savannah raised an eyebrow at Cara. "They're probably busy romping in the—"

"Okay," Cara snapped. "We get the picture. Besides, he's out of town."

"And how would you know?" Savannah asked.

Cara's eyes widened. "Isn't that what Lydia said? She can't keep him at home. It's no wonder he's gone all the time."

"What's your deal?" Savannah asked. "If they're getting along, and Dean's being nice to her, we should be happy for her. She's been miserable for too long. Lyds deserves some happiness."

Cara's lips curled downward. "Maybe there's a reason they haven't gotten along in a long time."

"Why are you hating on Lyds?" Savannah asked.

"I'm not," Cara said. "You know how she is—high maintenance."

Savannah pulled out a mirror and fixed her lipstick. "Dean knew what he was getting into when he married her."

"You would know that how?" Cara asked. "We didn't know them then."

"Hormones eating you up today?" Savannah asked. "She's not a delicate flower hiding her desires. They were a cute couple until they had problems getting pregnant."

"*Not* getting pregnant, you mean." Cara scowled.

"I give up," Savannah said. "It's probably better if she stays home today. If looks could kill, girl, you'd be the end of our friend."

"Okay, enough," Bri said. She looked between them, letting her gaze linger on Cara.

If Cara was going to act like that, she needed to at least tell Savannah why she was so irritated with Lydia. Did Cara have feelings for the father of her child? Had she lied about it being a one-time thing?

"How are things with Ethan, Cara? Is he excited about the baby?" Bri asked.

Cara shot Bri a dirty look.

"Now you're mad at Bri?" Savannah asked. "Is there a way to get those hormones in check? I don't want to be next."

Cara's lips formed a straight line. "I suppose I'm edgy because of the pregnancy."

"How are things with Ethan?" Bri asked again.

"Fine. Why do you ask?" Cara narrowed her eyes.

Bri narrowed her eyes back.

"What's going on?" Savannah asked. "I'm beginning to think I'm out of the loop on something."

"You going to tell her, too?" Bri asked, unable to keep the irritation out of her voice.

"Looks like I have to now," Cara said. "But I thought we were going to keep this between us. Remember our *deal*?"

"Our deal that I wouldn't say anything to *Lydia*?" Bri asked.

"Details," muttered Cara.

"Huh?" Savannah asked. "Just tell me."

Cara picked up her glass of sparkling water and took a long sip.

Savannah gave Bri a questioning look.

Bri shook her head, tired of Cara's attitude. "Want me to tell her? That might be easier."

Cara slammed her glass down and stared at Savannah. "Turns out

Ethan can't father a child. Happy?"

Savannah choked on her water. "What? Who…?"

"And it turns out Lydia's the one in *her* relationship who can't have kids." Cara sat taller, anger covering her face.

"You mean…?" Savannah dropped her fork onto the plate.

Others turned to their table.

"How could you do that to Lydia?" Savannah whispered. "I thought you two were getting even closer because you both had the fertility issues."

Cara's face softened somewhat. "Look, I didn't mean for it to happen. You're right, though. We were getting closer. After I found out about Ethan's infertility, before even telling him the news, I went straight to Lydia's house to talk. She was out, but Dean was in. One thing led to another…I'm sure you can figure out the rest."

"You're not still seeing him?" Savannah asked.

A strange look covered Cara's face. "A few times. You know how infrequently he's home."

Bri leaned over the table. "Yet he's been in town more often lately. Is that a coincidence?"

Cara stirred her drink. She looked conflicted.

"You've told us this much," Bri said. "We're not going to say anything to anyone."

"Sometimes he does see me before going home or to the airport." Cara continued to stare at her water.

"What does that mean? I thought it was a one-time deal."

Cara's face grew red. "I don't want to talk about it."

"What about Ethan?" Bri asked.

"He finds me disgusting, remember?"

"How could you?" Savannah demanded.

"It had nothing to do with her. Dean—"

"Nothing to do with her?" Savannah glared at Cara. "They're married, and she's your *friend*. It has everything to do with her. She was crushed about not being able to have kids with him. It nearly ruined their marriage."

"Marriage?" Cara exclaimed. "Dean travels to stay away from her. He jumped at the job opening."

"How long have you been seeing him?" Bri asked, suddenly understanding she didn't have the whole story. Probably not even close.

Cara folded her arms. "Since I found out about Ethan shooting blanks." Cara looked around, clearly aware of the attention they were drawing.

"Where are you at now?" Savannah asked. "Would you consider yourself in a relationship with him?"

"Am I on trial?" Cara's face turned redder.

"Lydia isn't here to defend herself," Bri said. "Someone has to."

"Both of you?" Cara asked.

"If the situation was reversed, we'd do the same thing to her," Savannah said. "That's not how you treat a friend, and I thought we were tight."

"And I doubt Lydia would do that." Bri folded her arms.

"Seriously?" Cara stared at her. "She had a long-term affair with a married man. We don't know who—she never told any of us. For all we know, it was one of our husbands."

"It wasn't," said Bri.

Savannah's eyes widened. "What's with all the secrets? I thought we were close. Now I feel like I don't know *any* of you."

"I just found out last night at the meeting," Bri said. "I caught her staring at him."

"Who was it?" Savannah asked. "Did you confirm?"

"Wouldn't you like to know?" Bri asked. "It doesn't affect any of us—trust me. They're not close to us. I doubt we've said more than a casual greeting to them."

Savannah looked both irritated and deep in thought. "Guess I'll have to ask Lydia myself."

"Watch her at the next meeting. I didn't mean to figure it out, but she kind of made it obvious. She can't let go."

"With Dean right there?" Cara looked disgusted. "They walk in holding hands, and she can't keep her eyes off someone else's husband? Whore."

"What?" Exclaimed Bri. "Take that back."

"Never. I can't believe she would do that to Dean."

"You're one to talk," Savannah said, her lips curling down. "Showing up with Ethan, but carrying Dean's baby."

Cara's nostrils flared. "Not so loud. If he wasn't there, it would be different. They were holding hands and everything."

Anger built up in Bri's stomach. "You're such a hypocrite, Cara."

"Watch it," Cara warned. "Don't forget that I have stuff on you. Both of you."

"Looks like we're on equal ground now. Aren't we?" Bri leaned over the table in Cara's direction. "You can stop holding our secret over our heads. We could go to Ethan at any minute."

Cara snorted. "Right. Then I rat the two of you out, and I know you don't want that."

Bri looked over at Savannah, who was pale. She mumbled something. It sounded like not wanting to go to jail.

"What?" Bri exclaimed.

"Nothing." Savannah turned to Cara. "Do I need to keep an eye out on Tom, too? Are you going to make your rounds?"

"Seriously?" Cara asked. "You're going there?"

"I have to ask." Savannah folded her arms. "Is my husband next on your list?"

"I'm married and carrying someone else's baby. Do you really think I want to get involved with anyone else?"

"Good, because you're not Tom's type. I'm his type, and he's very happy with me, so don't even consider it." Savannah flipped back her hair.

"He's hardly my type, either," Cara said, turning her nose up. "I'm more into bankers than bikers."

Bri pulled out her phone and called Lydia again. "Still not answering."

"Maybe she knows." Savannah stared at Cara. "Would she have any reason to suspect?"

Cara's face lost color. "No."

"Right," said Savannah. "She's probably too busy with Dean in the bedroom to worry about you. I'm sure that right now she's got her hands all over—"

"I'm not putting up with this anymore," Cara said. "If you two can't at least be nice to me, then I'll find someone else to hang out with. There's a whole group of pregnant ladies in the HOA. I'm sure they'd be more than happy to hang out with me."

"You want to start hanging out with them, dear?" Bri asked, allowing as much sarcasm in her voice as possible.

"What's wrong with them?" Cara narrowed her eyes.

"Only that they're about half our age," Savannah said.

"Half our age?" Cara exclaimed. "Hardly. That would put us at practically fifty. Stop exaggerating."

"They can't be more than twenty-two or twenty-three," Bri said. "Fresh out of college and ready to start their families."

"Yeah," Cara said, "and none of us are even close to planning our fortieth birthday parties. They're not even close to half our age."

"Then why haven't you started hanging out with them already?" Bri asked.

Cara pressed her palms against the table. "Do you guys want to get rid of me? Stop being friends because of this? I didn't do anything to Lydia. She can't stand Dean. We all know that. And like I said, I didn't *mean* for this to happen."

"Well that makes everything all right then, doesn't it?" asked Savannah.

"What about all the times after that initial oops?" Bri asked. "Did you mean for those to happen? Or do you just have no self-control?"

Cara glared at them. "Actually, I didn't mean to, at least not at first." Cara looked genuine. "Dean stopped by when Ethan was at work, and I was going to tell him about the baby, but he actually started ranting about Lydia wanting a family. He was really pissed, so I knew telling him was a bad idea. I didn't think we'd keep seeing each other, but he kept showing up, and Ethan has made it clear how gross he thinks I am now that I'm pregnant. Would you turn down someone who wants to love you when going home to that?"

"Honey, it's not love," Bri said. "Whatever Dean feels for you, that's not it."

"You know what I mean."

Savannah shook her head. "I just can't believe you'd do that to Lydia."

"If she was still with mystery man, she wouldn't care. Neither would you."

"Then why not tell her?" asked Bri.

"Really? Really?" Cara exclaimed. She looked Bri in the eyes and then Savannah. "Just let me deal with this, all right? I'll find out what's going on between Dean and Lydia, and then go from there."

Searching

LYDIA SAT IN the back of the quiet coffee shop setting up the new laptop. It was slow, and a bit of a clunker, but it would do the job. She was only going to use it for the purpose of trying to figure out what Dean was hiding.

She set it up with the pen name she used for work, and chose a password that Dean would never guess. It was a secret between Lydia and her best friend in junior high—and she doubted that Sheila Cramer would try to get into the laptop. Lydia and Sheila had created some elaborate stories about their future marriages. They had laid out every detail, down to the names of their ideal spouses and imaginary kids. The password was her dream husband's name along with the names of the kids Lydia would never have.

Then Lydia set up a fake email account, this time not using her pen name. It couldn't be anything that linked back to her in any way. She went with the middle name of her imaginary daughter and Sheila's imaginary son's name as the last name: Ashley Jacoby. That would be easy enough to remember, but no one would have a reason to link it to her.

Lydia had spent so much time thinking about the clippings, she had most of the names and places memorized. She powered off her phone, not wanting the distraction, but also not wanting Dean to be able to track her. She knew she was probably being paranoid, but would rather be safe. Chances were that Dean still didn't care where she went or what she did. Even when he was gone for weeks at a time, he never bothered to call and check in.

Or maybe he didn't because he knew exactly where she was. He purchased the phones, and just like everything else, those were in his name. It would probably take little effort to find her location and even who she was calling.

Lydia slid down into the chair, balancing the laptop on her stomach. How had she been so stupid? Of course that's what Dean was doing. He probably knew every move she made, and he probably knew all about her magazine job that she had gone to so much effort to keep from him.

It was probably the fact that none of that money went into their household that he didn't say anything. She was working, but not because he was a failure.

Lydia sat back up. She would have to be more careful with this computer, not giving Dean any way to get inside. She set the browser to private and typed in the name of the most recent murder victim: Jessica Aldridge, a librarian from Houston. There wasn't much more online about the killing than had been in the clipping.

She looked for social media profiles, finding all of them private. Of course. Jessica probably taught everyone who came into her library all about Internet safety. She was probably a stickler for it herself.

There were ways around that. Lydia set up a profile for Ashley Jacoby, setting it to private. Lydia found a free stock photo of a woman by a lake with the sun shining so her face was completely washed out. She looked around for people with open profiles and thousands of friends. Those were the types who accepted requests blindly.

Within a half an hour Lydia—Ashley—had a legit profile complete with a couple hundred friends and more accepting requests every couple of minutes. She added some more free stock photos and even went as far as tagging some of her new "friends" in the pictures. Only one guy rejected the tag.

Lydia smiled. Aside from the fact that the profile was just created, it looked completely legit. She interacted with some of the new friends, commenting on their statuses and photos. Then she posted some links, photos, and funny statuses which all took up space on her profile page. If someone scrolled down, they would believe she had years' worth of stuff.

She found Jessica's profile again. Lydia sent a friend request followed by a private message: *Hi Jess. Not sure if you remember me. It's been so long since we were in that one class together. What was it? History of the written word? Anyway, I just stumbled across your page and wanted to say hi. Maybe catch up. I don't know how we ever lost touch, but it would be great to hear from you. Talk soon. -Ashley.*

Lydia hit send. Obviously she didn't expect a response from Jessica, but a friend or family member probably had access to the profile, and hopefully they would contact her.

She waited a few minutes, responding to her new friends who had commented on her stuff. It could be a while before she heard back from one of Jessica's relatives, so Lydia opened a new tab and looked for more information on another victim. The one before Jessica was Sarah Troff, a hotel manager from San Diego.

There was a lot more on her than Jessica. Sarah had not only news articles, but a website had been created dedicated to finding her killer. Lydia wondered if Dean knew about that. She scrolled through the main page, which mostly explained what the news articles had. Nobody really knew how she had been killed. It was being investigated as suspicious circumstances.

The site was set up to accept comments, of which there were hundreds. Some thought that it might have been an undetectable poison. Others thought she might have been scared and died from fright because she had a heart condition. Others had even more exotic ideas, but the thing that was clear was no one knew for sure, and most believed foul play.

Lydia went to the About page, and skimmed the long post about Sarah's life. She paid more attention to the pictures scattered throughout. Sarah had been very pretty, and Lydia couldn't help noticing that she looked similar to herself, only blonde. Come to think of it, Jessica had similar features to Lydia. Dark hair in a similar style and a build much like hers. Obviously Dean had a type.

Going through the various pages on the site, Lydia noticed several names showing up over and over. Those would be good people to add to her new social media account. Lydia switched tabs and added about ten people. In the short time she'd been looking at Sarah's page, nearly another hundred people had accepted her requests.

Lydia interacted with some of them for a few minutes. It was actually kind of fun pretending to be someone else. She wasn't sure if it was because of the stress or not. In a way, her job was the same thing since she used a pen name. She smiled at a joke someone posted, and went to leave a comment.

"What's so funny?"

Lydia jumped and closed the laptop. She looked up to see Cara. "Don't scare me like that." Lydia felt like her heart was pounding out of her chest. "What are doing here?"

Cara shrugged and sat across from Lydia. "No one could get together today, so I decided to come here for refreshment." Cara took a sip from an iced tea and looked at Lydia's computer. "What are you doing? Why the cheap laptop?"

"This?" Lydia held it up, feeling like an idiot. How was she going to explain that?

"Yeah. The one you're holding." Cara arched an eyebrow.

"I didn't want to risk anything happening to my other one, so I thought I'd get one to take when I went out," Lydia lied.

Cara put a hand on her belly and rubbed. "Interesting. You're pretty jumpy over a cheap computer."

Lydia forced a sheepish expression. "Well, I didn't want anyone seeing me use something so inexpensive. You won't say anything will you?"

"Me? Of course not. I'm the keeper of secrets."

"So am I." Lydia grabbed her coffee and took a sip. "Is Ethan being any nicer?"

"Toward me?" Cara laughed bitterly. "Hardly. You know what? After all this crap, I've lost what respect I did have for him. There's no way I can look at him the same again. Not after the things he's said to me."

Lydia thought about some of the horrible things Dean had said to her over the years. "I can understand that. Why not leave?"

"Why stay with Dean?" Cara leaned forward, staring at Lydia. She seemed to be asking more than she spoke.

Lydia squirmed in the seat. "We're getting along better now. You saw us the other night at the meeting."

Cara leaned even closer. "But how can you forget everything that's happened between you? I could never forget some of the things he's said to you. All those affairs."

Lydia stared at her, trying to figure out what Cara's angle was. She seemed upset that Lydia was getting along with Dean. Was she jealous because Ethan was being so terrible toward her?

Cara sat up straight. "I just don't want to see you get hurt."

"I can take care of myself."

"Good to hear." Cara glanced up at a clock. "I'd better get going. I have an appointment to get to."

"Okay. Nice running into you."

"Always." Cara smiled sweetly. "Maybe see you tomorrow?"

"Perhaps."

Lydia watched as Cara walked out of the coffee shop. She couldn't shake the feeling that there was something more to the conversation than appeared. She chalked it up to hormones or Cara being on edge over the state of her marriage.

Lydia went back to the laptop. She checked to see if anyone related to the murdered women had accepted her requests yet. They hadn't. She went to a page that had pictures of Sarah that her friends had uploaded to the site and studied the pictures. Lydia wasn't sure what she was looking for, but found them interesting.

Some of the images were from various press conferences and others were of the crime scene—after it had been cleaned up. There were also pictures of her home and work. Her friends and family had left no stone left unturned. If any of his victims' families were going to uncover anything incriminating, it would likely be this one.

It was too bad they were all the way in San Diego. Lydia would love to go there herself and poke around. But following the site and trying to make friends with Sarah's friends would have to do.

Lydia pulled out her phone and scanned the list of victims. One of the older cases was in Oregon. That wasn't too far away. She could probably find an excuse to go there.

She put her phone back in her purse and typed the Oregon victim's name into the search bar. There was a long list of articles. The first two pages were all news articles. There weren't any pages like Sarah Troff had—at least nothing Lydia could find. She clicked on a random news link. The details were the same as the clipping.

Lydia scanned the images and froze. At a press conference, Dean stood in the audience. Lydia blinked several times, her pulse on fire. Without a doubt it was her husband.

He had been careless.

That meant that he had probably been careless in other ways too. This wasn't enough evidence to incriminate him, but it was a start. Lydia saved the image to the computer and bookmarked the link. Then just to be safe, she took a screen shot of the entire article. It was an obscure news source and she couldn't risk it disappearing before she went to the cops.

Travels

LYDIA STEPPED OUT of her car into the scorching heat. She looked across the parking lot and considered parking closer for a minute. She decided against it because she needed to keep her car hidden. It was underneath a tree in between two large trucks. No one would notice it there.

Heat assaulted her from both the sun above and the pavement below. It felt like she had traveled across the country, not one state away—still in the Pacific Northwest. She had just entered Oregon, and as soon as she got into the coffee shop she was going to check and see if she had gotten any more messages.

The bag carrying the laptop rubbed against her leg, making her all the more uncomfortable. Oregon was having a heat wave while Seattle and the surrounding areas had cooler than average temperatures. That made the heat wave even worse. She wasn't acclimated in the slightest.

Lydia opened the door to the coffee shop and stood just inside the entry, taking in the air conditioning. She ordered an iced tea and then made herself comfortable near the back. Lydia pulled out her laptop and once the clunker started, she checked her online profile. She had a couple dozen new friends, but no messages from anyone who knew the Oregon victim.

Jen Pittman had turned up missing on Halloween the previous year and had been found a week later in some woods by teenagers. Jen had been a flight attendant, spending most of her free time in Hollywood but had been expected at a friend's Halloween party.

Even though Lydia couldn't get any of Jen's friends or family to write back, she had been able to hunt down a couple addresses. So Lydia would be Ashley Jacoby, the flight attendant.

Since there were no new messages, Lydia double checked the addresses she had written down as she finished off the tea. Everything was in order, just like her story. She was ready, although not excited about spending another hour in the car. Her butt was already numb. But at least the car was cool.

Lydia logged off and shut down the computer. She looked around the coffee shop as the laptop took its time. Everyone was just living their lives. Some looked frazzled, but even so, Lydia envied them. They all appeared to have normal lives. Her life had been far from normal for too long, and now here she was investigating murders that she thought her husband might be behind.

How had everything come to this? Back when they first got married, it seemed that she had the world at her fingertips. She thought anything was possible, and that all her dreams would come true. Her entire body had buzzed with excitement for what the future held for her.

Everyone had been talking to her about the wedding and honeymoon, but Lydia couldn't stop thinking about having a bunch of little Deans running around at their feet. They both wanted three kids, maybe four if the first three were all boys or girls. They had spent hours talking about what their life would be like.

When her friends complained about their fiancés and avoided talking about kids, Dean had been more than eager. He wanted to coach soccer like his dad had for him. He couldn't wait to take them camping. Dean's eyes had lit up when talking about teaching his kids to fish and then prepare the meat.

The one thing they hadn't discussed was what would happen if they couldn't have kids. It hadn't crossed either of their minds—at least not Lydia's. If Dean had thought about it, he hadn't said anything. But that had changed everything, and Dean didn't want to adopt. He wasn't going to raise someone else's kid.

Lydia had tried to explain that wasn't the way adoption worked. The children would become their own, but he wouldn't hear anything about it. He cited cases where biological parents had come to rip kids away from their loving, adoptive families. He wouldn't risk having that happen.

Had that been the start of his killing spree? Lydia didn't know if the papers in the box were the full story. They only went back a couple years. She had already hooked up with Chad by then, which meant that Dean had pulled away from her a while before that. How long? Lydia tapped her finger, calculating the difference.

It had to have been at least six months before Chad since Dean had gone near Lydia in a romantic kind of way. But would their inability to have a baby be enough reason for him to start this? It was a really extreme way to deal with it—to put it mildly. Cheating would have made sense, and that's why Lydia had suspected it and eventually gone in that direction herself.

Not that she'd set out to, but after she ran into Chad practically every day in different locations around town it seemed like that was who fate...or some other force...was guiding her toward. So she had struck up a conversation with him one day when she ran into him at lunch. She usually talked with people easily, but Chad was an entirely different case. After only five minutes, they both felt like they were talking with someone they'd known for a lifetime, and since they were both really frustrated with their marriages, one thing led to another pretty quickly.

Lydia shook her head to clear it. It wasn't the time to think about Chad. All it took was trying to figure out a date when Dean might have changed, and she was gushing over Chad... again.

He was controlling and could be a jerk when he didn't get his own way. But wasn't that just the way men were? They could be nice and tell the ladies everything they want to hear, but then once they got what they wanted, everything changed. It was just a man thing, and most guys didn't kill people.

Lydia stood up and headed for her car. She would have to think more about his behavior while she drove. Even if she did find something that should have told her what was going on, what good would it do to know now? She had obviously missed anything that had already been there.

She turned on the car, cranked the AC, and then scrolled through the upcoming directions on the GPS to give herself an idea of what was coming up. It was mostly a straight shot with only a few turns before she got to Jen's town.

While she drove, Lydia couldn't help going over everything she could remember about Dean. Aside from his frequent travels—that everyone always commented on—there wasn't anything she could think of that would have given her any reason to believe something sinister was going on.

Sure, he was gone a *lot,* but that just pointed to how driven he was with work and how unhappy he was at home. Lydia couldn't give him the one thing he wanted, so he didn't want to be around her. That was hardly rocket science.

What about his childhood? That was something he rarely talked about, even when Lydia asked questions. His dad expected perfection. A test score of ninety-eight percent wasn't good enough. The man refused to give any praise even when Dean did score perfectly, which had been often.

Dean had often quoted his father's response to a perfect test score. "You expect me to praise you for what you're supposed to be doing?" Dean's voice always held the same amount of smugness each time when he mimicked his father, so it was clear that he'd heard it a lot even though eventually he'd stopped trying to get approval from his dad.

Maybe whatever Dean didn't talk about from his past had contributed to him becoming a murderer. Lydia was pretty sure that having an impossible to please parent didn't drive people to become psychopaths. It probably didn't help to prevent it, but it couldn't cause it. Or could it?

Her parents had expected a lot out of her, but they weren't jerks about it. And then when her mom's health began to fail, they paid even less attention, barely noticing when she struggled with a subject.

Could it be something in his genes? She didn't know of any of Dean's relatives in either jail or psychiatric care. All of his relatives were accounted for, working long hours to be able to compete with each other. His family gatherings were always full of competition—whose car was the most expensive, whose house had the most square feet, whose vacation destination was the most luxurious. It gave her headaches.

It usually made her miss her mom. Things were so simple, yet so painful, when it came to her. Her mom had once been a strong woman with a huge personality. Seeing her stuck to a bed in need of twenty-four hour nursing care ripped her heart out. It was even worse that she couldn't see her very often, but at least her mom knew and appreciated the fact that Lydia had her job for the magazine to pay for her care.

Lydia would have to make a point to visit her mom again after she got back home. Dean was due back soon, but once he left again, she needed to visit her mom. It had been too long, and distance really wasn't an excuse even if her mom had no concept of time anymore.

The GPS told her to exit the freeway, so she pulled over to the off ramp and stopped trying to psychoanalyze Dean. She had to focus on getting to the addresses she had. One was Jen's sister and the other two were friends. She had decided to start with the sister, thinking that she might know more. It might be a long shot either way.

When she got to the address, she drove down a little farther and parked in front of a neighbor's house underneath a weeping willow with branches so low they nearly touched her car. She cracked the windows and then turned the car off.

Lydia checked her mirror. Her hair was pulled back in a messy bun which was a way she never wore it and she had done her makeup differently too. She had gone with thicker eyeliner and twice the mascara. She pulled out never-used tube of bright red lipstick. It had been a gift from Savannah who thought Lydia would look gorgeous with darker lips. Lydia knew from experience that most shades of red lip color made her look like Snow White's evil stepmother.

Hopefully with her hair back, the red lips wouldn't have the same effect. She put it on and had to stare at herself for a moment. She barely looked like herself, and she thought about wiping it all off but she knew better. Even though she wasn't trying to be completely disguised, she wanted to look different. She had accomplished that.

She looked in the side mirror and caught sight of someone leaving the house she watching. The woman headed for a car parked across the street. It was time for action.

Home

CARA FOLDED THE last box and jammed it into the recycle canister, forcing it in and closing the lid. Hopefully, Dean didn't have anything to recycle, because if he did it wasn't going to fit. She went back into the house pretending not to see the neighbors watching her.

They weren't the friendliest bunch. Back in her neighborhood—her *old* neighborhood—people were…well, neighborly. When someone moved in, it was almost a contest to see who could meet the new people first. Bonus points if you brought a meal that they liked or they invited you in.

Not here. The houses were even more beautiful, and the lake so gorgeous. Dean's new house was across the street and had a view to die for.

Cara wanted to bring the girls over to see, but she hadn't even told anyone that she had moved out. And they would probably tell Lydia, anyway. Dean would be pissed if she found out. He'd managed to keep his condo a secret from her all that time.

When she had packed her things into the moving truck, Cara discovered that it wasn't a moving truck. His friend had brought a truck with a huge logo of a charity on every side. The neighbors probably thought they were donating a bunch of stuff, and no doubt had been proven right when Ethan moved in the furniture to replace what Cara had taken.

No one would ask any questions.

Cara closed the front door and looked around. Even though she had filled the truck, the house was sparse. She had barely packed enough things to fill an apartment—a small one. The previous owners had also left things dirty and messy. She'd had to scrub the fridge, but at least they'd left one.

The main bathroom was what she had put off, but now it was the only thing left. Dean was due back soon and she wanted the house to be nice when he saw it for the first time. The ones he had actually looked at in person had already been purchased. It was no wonder this one hadn't been, but once she cleaned the gross messes, it was beautiful.

She went upstairs and stood by the largest window in the house, the one that overlooked the lake. There was also a deck, which Cara found odd since it was in the front of the house, but that was where the view was. She didn't feel like having any of the neighbors watch her, so she leaned against the window sill and watched the waves.

After a while, some kids ran into the water, disrupting the wave pattern. She could hear their squeals and shouts through the window. She watched for a few more minutes until her lower back started to ache.

Cara went into the bedroom and looked at the bed—the one that had been in the guest room at *Ethan's* house. It had never really been her house. Not with the prenuptial. How had she ever been so naive to think that she could have truly had a happily ever after when she had to sign one of those?

Ethan's parents didn't trust her because of where she was from, but that didn't mean he had to listen to them by agreeing to the form. Was he glad that he had?

Tears stung at her eyes. She really hadn't meant to hurt him, and after that first time with Dean, Cara had promised herself that she would never go back to him. But then after she told Dean about the pregnancy, she couldn't stop herself. Was it because of the excitement or knowing that her baby was his?

Why hadn't Ethan confronted her? Asked her about it? For all he knew, a miracle had occurred and he had been treated his wife like trash. Why hadn't she thought to say that when she was arguing with him?

Cara took a deep breath. It didn't matter anymore. It was over, and she was starting over with Dean.

Or was she? Was he only letting her stay there? If he planned on staying with Cara to start a family, would he end it with Lydia? Or would he lead a double life?

Cara leaned back against the pillow and closed her eyes. She repositioned herself, trying to ease the back pain, but it wasn't helping. It seemed to get worse, actually. And that wasn't the only thing that hurt, either. She stretched her legs and arms. Everything below her neck and above her waist hurt—or at least that's how it felt. She was only about halfway, so it was bound to only get worse.

Her heavy eyelids finally helped her to fall asleep. Cara's body felt better as she drifted off. A smile tugged at her lips as the warm sleepiness overtook everything.

The sound of the front door opening woke Cara. She sat up in a groggy stupor, confused at first. Then she remembered that Dean was back in town and the real estate agent had left the keys at his office for him after meeting Cara when she moved in.

She stretched and tried to pull herself out of the mental fog, but found herself stuck. She must have been in the middle of a really deep sleep.

Dean was downstairs, walking around. She could hear his shoes tapping on the hardwood floors. Cara tried to get off the bed, but her body refused to cooperate. She had imagined greeting him at the door with a big hug and an even bigger kiss. So much for that.

Cara slapped her right cheek and then her left. It didn't help. She was going to be groggy when she saw Dean, and there was nothing she could do about it.

He appeared in the doorway and smiled when he looked at her. "Did I wake you?"

"I was busy cleaning. I wanted it to be nice when you got here."

Dean shook his head. "I told you to wait. I would take care of the messes. Or better yet, hire the housekeeper to come here, too."

"Like I said, I didn't want you to come home to that." Cara stretched again. "Besides, wouldn't you worry about the maid saying something to Lydia?"

"She knows who signs her checks. Just relax." He rubbed his palm across her forehead.

Cara closed her eyes. It was so nice to be with Dean. To be taken care of.

"You're so cute when you're tired." He kicked his shoes off and slid into the bed next to her and wrapped his arms around her. "How are you and my baby?" He rubbed her stomach.

Cara's heart fluttered and she opened her eyes. "We're good. Just tired."

He placed his lips on hers. "Let's rest then. I'm tired from the plane ride, too." He helped her to lean back, keeping his arm around her. "You must be tired if the house was in half as bad of shape as you told me. I didn't see a speck of dirt anywhere."

"Good." Cara rubbed the back of his hand. "That's what I wanted."

"Where did you learn to clean like that? I've only seen professionals that meticulous."

"It's not a big deal." From a young age, Cara had been cleaning worse messes. Her mom had gone through more boyfriends than she could count, and most of them had been abusive drunks. They often left a trail of broken items and blood before they passed out or stumbled out to the yard to pick a fight with a neighbor.

More times than she could count, Cara had cleaned up after them so her mom wouldn't have to. Not just that, but she didn't want her mom to see how bad it really was. Since leaving home, Cara wished she hadn't done so much to protect her mom—what she needed was to see how things really were and wake up.

Dean pulled some of Cara's hair away from her face. "What are you thinking about?"

"Nothing. I'm just glad to be here with you." At least he didn't treat women like her mom's boyfriends.

"Mmm. Me too." He kissed her again. "Hey...was that the baby?"

Cara had forgotten that his hand was still on her stomach. "Yeah. When I rest, he parties."

"He?"

"It's better than saying 'it.'"

He sat up and rubbed both hands around her belly. "There it is again."

"Like I said, a real party animal." Warmness ran through Cara as she watched Dean's expressions when he felt the baby move.

"That's really something. How long has this been going on?"

"On the outside? Not too long. I should probably write this stuff down. It's hard to remember everything. But I'm just not the journaling type."

"Don't worry about it, then. No need to add anything else for you to worry about."

"But I need a job and health insurance and—"

"You just need to take care of yourself, darling. This place is your home, and I'll leave one of my credit cards. Get groceries online if you want. Consider the insurance taken care of. I'll add you to my policy. I'm sure Ethan's will still cover you through month's end, no matter how unhappy that makes him."

Cara's entire body relaxed at the news. "That's such a relief. Thank you, Dean."

"What else would you expect?"

"I wasn't sure what you would do, to be honest. I mean, this is obviously not the ideal situation."

He shook his head. "That it's not, but I know how to make the best of something that on the surface looks bad. That's how I've managed to work my way through the company and get where I'm at."

Cara leaned her head against Dean's shoulder. "Thank you." She snuggled closer, glad to finally feel taken care of by someone.

Incognito

LYDIA HURRIED ACROSS the street before the lady got inside the car. She was glad she chose sensible shoes, because her heels wouldn't have helped her, especially in this heat.

"Wait!"

The woman turned toward Lydia, her hazel eyes widening.

"Are you Jen's sister? Angela?"

"What do you want?" she asked, answering the question.

Lydia stopped about two feet in front of her. "I'm Ashley. I was a friend of Jen's in flight attendant training. We were supposed to meet up for old times' sake not long ago, and then when she didn't show I did some digging and found out what happened."

Angela's eyes narrowed. "Why are you here? Are you the one trying to friend me on Facebook?"

"I am. I need to know what happened to my friend. It was such a shock to hear what happened."

"You keep saying 'what happened,' but you can say it. She was killed—murdered, actually."

Lydia bit her lip. "I'm really sorry for your loss. Do you have time to talk with me?"

"If you didn't notice, I'm heading out now. How did you find my home address anyway?"

"Phone book."

Angela's eyebrows came together. "I'm not in it."

"Well, I'm sorry to say, but you're in several online."

"Why do they keep doing this? I keep telling those people to keep my information off their sites."

Lydia took a step back. "I'm sorry for bothering you. I just wanted to find out what happened with Jen." She turned around.

"Okay."

Was it really that easy? Lydia turned back around slowly. "You'll speak with me?"

"I'll meet you at that Mexican restaurant near Fourth and Stewart in an hour. You know where that is?"

"No, but I'll find it."

Angela unlocked her car with a remote and got in, not looking at Lydia.

Lydia went back to her car and watched Angela drive away in the rear view mirror. When she was out of sight, Lydia put the cross-street into the GPS and saw that it was only a few minutes away. Lydia turned on the car and then blasted the AC. Just standing in the sun for those few short minutes almost had her in a sweat.

She was about to pull out into the street when someone tapped a window on the passenger side. Lydia looked over to see a girl who didn't look old enough to be out of college. She had thick, curly red hair falling into her face. She indicated for Lydia to roll down the window.

Lydia did. "Yes?"

"Were you asking about Jen?"

"Yeah. You knew her?"

She nodded. "What do you want to know?"

"I'm trying to find out what happened. You know, more than what's online."

"Yeah, totally. Come to my house, and I'll tell you what I know."

It almost seemed too easy, but Lydia would take it. "Okay." She cut the engine and got out of the car. "Some heat wave, huh?"

The girl smiled. "I love it. My name's Tessa." She held out her hand.

Lydia took it and shook. "Ashley."

"Come on." Tessa led Lydia to a house across the street. It was a split level, like all of the two-stories in the neighborhood. The rest were quaint little ramblers.

It reminded Lydia of the neighborhood some of her friends from school had lived in when she was younger. Lydia had loved getting away from the trailer park to spend time in a real house for a while.

Tessa opened the door and the smell of ramen noodles hit Lydia.

"I just made some lunch. Hungry?" Tessa asked, closing the door behind them.

"No thanks. Want me to take my shoes off?"

Tessa looked at her like Lydia was an alien. "Why? Come on in. Hope you don't mind if I eat in front of you."

"Go ahead." Lydia looked at the pictures that covered the walls. It looked like a typical happy suburban family. She could have been walking into the house of any of her friends from childhood. She wanted to get into Angela's house and see if she could get more ideas about what Jen's life had been like.

Lydia sat at the kitchen table. Tessa poured the steaming noodles from a pot into a bowl and then sat across from Lydia. "Jen used to babysit me, and then I walked her dog when I got older. Angie kept the dog when she was out of town, which was like all the time."

"Where's the dog now?"

"No one knows." Tessa slurped some noodles, one splashing onto her nose.

Lydia raised an eyebrow. "How's that?"

"Brittney disappeared the same time Jen was killed. She probably had the dog with her and she ran away after Jen... well, you know. When she was killed."

"Did Jen take the dog with her a lot?"

Tessa shrugged. "Sometimes."

"What do you think happened?" Lydia asked. "Was she seeing someone?"

"She was talking about some guy named Doug for a while, but he was at night school taking a test when she went missing, so he didn't do it."

"Do you have any theories?" Lydia leaned back in the chair, trying to act as natural as she could.

"Probably someone she met through work. She traveled the world, and she loved staying in different places. Jen always told me how exciting it was to meet so many different types of people. But you probably know all about that, right? I heard you say you were in school with her."

"Uh, I was laid off so I'm kind of in between jobs at the moment. That's why I was going to hang out with Jen when I did."

"It took you this long to find her family?"

Lydia's stomach twisted. She had obviously not put enough thought into the story if a college kid was able to find the holes so easily. "Well, I didn't want to bother anyone at first. If one of my relatives were murdered, I wouldn't want random people she knew contacting me. So I waited."

Tessa slurped some more noodles. "That makes sense. Yeah, they haven't wanted to talk with anyone about it. If anyone says anything about Jen to Angie, she runs off. She barely talks to me. I don't know, I think it just hurts to think about her. That's how I'd feel, I guess."

Lydia nodded. "I can see that. It'll be interesting to see what she has to say when I meet with her. That Doug guy, did you meet him?"

"No, but the cops talked to him. They weren't serious, and there was a whole class full of people who were with him the whole time. You know what I think?"

"What?"

"I think it's someone she met while traveling. I mean, if you think about it, it makes sense. Someone who was only here for a day or something would have the opportunity and means, and would be able to get out of town before anyone even knew what happened to her. Then no one would suspect him."

"Makes a lot of sense. You think it was a guy?"

Tessa pushed her empty bowl forward and then sat back. "I guess it could've been a girl, but they said the killer was strong. Like, really built. There was a huge struggle, and Jen was way overpowered."

Lydia leaned forward. "What happened? I couldn't find much online."

"It was at her condo, and it looked like they'd had a date. There was wine spilled on the couch and stuff. The cops didn't really say a lot. They were hoping to keep the details quiet so they could use them to nail whoever did it, but I don't think they'll ever find the guy. They couldn't find any prints, at least none that didn't belong. Jen's were everywhere, but she didn't snap her own neck, you know."

Lydia flinched. "That's how she died? Broken neck?"

Sadness washed over Tessa's face. "Yeah."

"And there weren't any other clues? Nothing in her car?"

"It was still at the airport, so she drove home with the murderer."

Lydia shivered. "Not a smart move."

"Nope. Maybe she thought she knew the guy. Some people think it was someone who had traveled on her route enough times to make her trust him. Some smooth-talker with a nice smile or something. But none of her coworkers could think of anyone who fit that description." Tessa frowned.

They sat in silence for a few minutes. Dean certainly fit the description of the culprit, but what was Lydia supposed to do? She certainly didn't have enough to turn him in.

Tessa cleared her throat. "I wish I had more answers for you. There's nothing more I'd love than to find the guy and break his neck. But he knew what he was doing. He may as well have been a ghost for what he left behind."

"I'd like to catch him, too." Lydia looked at the time. "I'm supposed to meet Angie soon. Thanks, Tessa, for talking with me. I really appreciate it."

"Sure. It's good to talk about her. No one really wants to. Not anyone who actually knew her, anyway. Everyone else loves to gossip, but that's not the same. I don't want to gossip. She was my friend." Tears filled Tessa's eyes.

Lydia got up and wrapped her arms around the girl. "I'm sure they'll get him eventually. He can't hide forever."

"I hope you're right."

"I am." Lydia pulled out her phone. "What's your email address? Maybe we can write each other after I'm back home."

"Okay." Tessa told Lydia her email address, and Lydia then got back into her car to find the Mexican restaurant.

She arrived a few minutes early, so she sat in the car processing everything Tessa had told her. Dean had every opportunity to commit the act. He had been in town at exactly that time, and he would have had a car available to him. Most of the time, the company either rented a car for him or had one for the employees.

If none of the other flight attendants could think of anyone Jen had been flirting with, he obviously knew enough to keep everything low key so that no one would have remembered him.

The thought of him breaking Jen's neck and cleaning up after himself made her sick. Her stomach twisted into tight knots, making her feel as though she might be sick. Sure, Lydia knew about the killings already, but talking to someone who had known one of the victims was like smacking herself in the face with reality that more than likely the man she married had done this. Multiple times.

Nausea ran through Lydia like a wave. Lydia opened the door and threw up in a rhododendron bush next to the car.

She sat back down and pulled a couple tissues out of her purse to clean up her face. Then she grabbed a handful of mints and threw those in her mouth. Her stomach still heaved, but she had to keep everything together. Angie was going to be there any minute, and maybe she would be able to provide additional insight.

Lydia crunched the mints as she watched people walk into the restaurant. Just as she was about to pile more mints, she saw Angie walking toward the door.

Clues

"**A**RE YOU SURE you only want water, Ashley?"

Lydia nodded. "I'm feeling pretty sick about what happened to Jen. I can't stomach any food right now."

Angie sipped her margarita. "I couldn't eat for days after I found out. So, you really only just found out about her death?"

"Yeah. It's silly, but we had a pact. If we both didn't have a boyfriend in two years, then we agreed to fly to the city of love together and find ourselves a match."

"That sounds like Jen." The corners of Angie's mouth twitched, but didn't form a smile. "I take it you don't have a boyfriend?"

"Nope. I hadn't heard from Jen, so I wasn't sure if we'd be on or not. I thought I might have to take someone else to Paris with me, but then I found out what happened." Lydia made the saddest face she could muster without being overly dramatic.

Angie looked thoughtful. "How close were you two?"

"Obviously, not that close." Lydia frowned. "We just grew close back then, but we were sent on different flights after we started working and lost touch, you know?"

"It happens too easily," Angie agreed. "I had a close friend before having kids. We were tight—told each other everything—and then things got busy after having kids. I just assumed that she was doing fine like me, but then one day I heard that she was in hospice care. She had cancer, and it pretty much took her right away."

"That's horrible," Lydia said, feeling sick. "How are her kids?"

Angie looked out the window and shrugged. "I haven't been able to learn much from the grapevine. I didn't know her husband or kids, so I can't just call up and ask. Sounds like the kids have been passed around a lot between relatives."

Lydia frowned. "I'm sorry about your friend."

"Dying young sucks no matter how it happens."

"It sure does." Lydia sipped her water, and then they sat in silence until the waiter brought the food.

"Can you eat some of the chips and salsa at least?" Angie asked. "I don't really want to eat in front of you."

"No problem." Lydia picked up a chip and dipped it in the salsa. "So, do you know anything about Jen that isn't in the papers? I've read what I can find, but it's really bugging me. It feels like there's more to the story, but I don't know what."

"Are you some kind of private investigator?"

"Who would've hired me?" Lydia asked.

Angie shrugged. "You've got to understand, we've had all kinds of reporters and curious looky-loos bombarding my family. In a town like this, murder doesn't happen everyday. It shook up the whole community, and the only thing that really gives any of us any comfort is believing that it was someone Jen met while working—someone from far away."

"It does make more sense. We see people everyday from all over the world. A flight from Seattle can hold people from twenty different countries going to twice as many destinations."

"Is that what you think happened?" Angie gave Lydia a suspicious look.

"Like you said, it's a lot more likely." Lydia squirmed, still under Angie's distrusting gaze. "Did she have a boyfriend that you knew about? Or someone that she'd been seeing semi-seriously?"

"No. She wanted to meet someone that she could settle down with, she'd been hoping for someone within the airline who would understand her work schedule, but she never mentioned having met anyone."

"Do you think it could have been a one-night stand type of thing?"

Angie's eyes narrowed. "She wasn't that type of girl. I think if you really did know her, you wouldn't even ask that."

"I think you're in denial. Everyone is capable of a quick fling like that. Especially in our business."

"You need to go now."

"What?" Lydia exclaimed. "We've barely—"

"And I'm done. I'm not sure what your angle is, but I don't want to talk about my sister with you anymore."

"I want to find out what happened to her. If it happened to one flight attendant, it can happen to others. What if the guy who did this has been doing this to other women? Don't you want to put a stop to him?"

Angie's eye's narrowed. "Of course I do. If you know anything other than what you're telling me, why don't you let me in on it? I'm not going to hand over information to a random stranger—and that's all you are. And just so you know, you're the first—and last—one I've even given the time of day to."

"I did know her," Lydia lied so she could keep her cover. "But I do also know about other similar killings in other areas. I think someone who travels a lot is killing people in random locations in hopes to not get caught."

"How would you know that?" Angie demanded.

It was time for a new tactic. Lydia relaxed her face and then looked around, lowering her voice. "There have been a string of these killings in cities I've been in. I wouldn't have noticed, except that I usually watch the local news. They happen in places I've been, Angie—starting with someone I knew." Lydia took a deep breath. "I could be next."

Angie's face was hard to read, but appeared to soften. "Do you think you're being followed?"

Lydia leaned forward. "I'm not sure, but it seems like more than just a coincidence. Don't you think?"

"How do you know they're not just similar cases?"

"They're all isolated, or so the authorities think. Just some random killing of a girl who never bothered anyone, but worked in a place where she would have access to people who travel a lot."

"So it's not just flight attendants?" Angie asked, looking curious.

Lydia shook her head. "Whoever's doing this is being careful. No one would ever think to connect any of these."

"Why do you? What makes you think they're related? Did you ever stop to think that maybe they're not?"

"I wish more than anything that they weren't. But the facts stick out, making it impossible for me to ignore."

"Have you tried talking to the authorities?"

"Not yet. I need more. Some kind of proof that goes deeper than just what's been on the news and online. That's why I'm talking with you."

"What do you think I can tell you that will connect all the dots?"

"I doubt you can do that," Lydia said. "However, I was hoping that something you had to say could help somehow. Maybe something you don't think is important actually leads to one of the other cases. That would be more than I have now."

"If that's the case, you should hire an investigator. You're not a very good one."

Lydia couldn't hide her look of disgust. "Like I said, I'm not trying to be a PI. I just want to be able to find a link between the cases. Then we can not only put away the guy who did this to Jen, but keep him from ever doing this again. It's only a matter of time before he strikes again, and the longer he gets away with it, the more he's going to keep on killing people."

Angie took a bite and chewed slowly before speaking. "What do you think I can tell you that you don't already know?"

"I don't know, but there has to be something. A piece of evidence the police are holding back on because they think it could help solve the case if the public is left in the dark over it."

"See? That's why professionals are needed. Not an amateur like you. Look, I'm getting a massive headache. I need to take care of that and then think about everything you've said. Can I have your number to call you later?"

"Do you still have my friend request? You never replied, but if you didn't ignore it you can still send me a message."

"I think you sent me a message, didn't you?" Angie asked.

"Probably." Lydia knew she had, but she wasn't going to let Angie know.

"If I think of anything to tell you, I'll find your messages and get a hold of you that way."

Lydia nodded. "Okay, and I can do the same. If I find anything that I think would help Jen's case, I'll let you know too."

Angie nodded, and then Lydia got up and walked across the street to a park so Angie couldn't identify her car. She sat on a bench underneath a tree. It only took a minute or two before the heat swarmed her. She started to sweat and suddenly wished she had drunk more water while in the restaurant.

She kept her attention across the street, waiting for Angie to leave. Before long, her tongue was sticking to the roof of her mouth. Lydia would need something to drink soon, but she couldn't risk Angie taking down her plates. The last thing she needed was for anyone to start snooping around.

Who knew what he would do?

He could wind up killing both of them if he felt threatened. That was the last thing Lydia wanted, so she would wait until Angie left no matter how dry her throat grew. She pulled out her phone and scrolled through the pictures of the newspaper articles, while also keeping her attention on the parking lot across the street.

People came and went, but not Angie. Did she own the place? Was that why she had invited Lydia there? Or was she simply a slow eater?

She couldn't take the heat a moment longer, so she got up and headed back across the street to get something to drink from the restaurant.

When Lydia got inside, Angie was in the waiting area talking to some guy. They both stopped as soon as Lydia walked through.

"Ashley," Angie said. "What are you doing back?"

"I went to the park across the street to clear my head, but now I'm thirsty. I keep forgetting how hot it is out there."

Angie nodded. "I'm just on my way out. I'll see you around." She said goodbye to the guy next to her and went outside.

"You want a pop?" asked the guy Angie had spoken with. "I can get you one on the house. Any friend of Angie's is a friend of mine."

Keeping her focus on Angie, Lydia nodded. "That sounds great. Thank you."

Just as Angie drove off, a waiter brought Lydia a glass with brown, bubbling liquid. Lydia thanked him and drank it as fast as she could, not realizing just how thirsty she was until she tasted the root beer. She handed the glass to the next server who walked by, and then went back to her car.

If Angie knew the people who worked there, she could find out Lydia's plates if she really wanted to, but Lydia didn't care anymore. She just wanted to get home and figure out her next step. This trip had been nothing other than a waste of time. She hadn't learned anything that put Dean near Jen—aside from what she already had.

Tired

LYDIA SLAMMED THE trunk, more than ready to get inside, eat, and then relax. Maybe she would even invite the girls over to play cards on the porch while the sun went down. She'd spent more than enough time by herself recently, and now, especially after all the driving, Lydia knew she needed time with her girls.

She went straight for the fridge, but groaned when she opened it. She needed to go shopping. There weren't two ingredients she could throw together to make a meal.

Lydia went into the pantry and grabbed a few bottles and put them in the fridge to replace the one she'd just finished off. If Bri and the others could come over, they would easily need at least three bottles.

Her body ached from so much driving. The last thing she wanted was to drive to the store, but her stomach was on the verge of growling so she didn't have much choice.

"Just run in and grab the bare essentials." Lydia gripped the steering wheel and forced her body into motion. She was so tired that she thought about going back home and climbing into bed without eating.

The first thing she did when she got inside was to get an iced mocha from the stand outside. The caffeine helped to energize her as she walked along, throwing things in her basket. After she had it full, she headed over to the wine section to grab an extra bottle, just in case.

Lydia stood there deciding between a couple flavors of dessert wine when someone bumped into her.

"Sorry," she said, even though she hadn't done anything.

"No, it's my fault." Lydia knew that voice anywhere.

She turned and looked at Chad. They stared at each other for a moment before she finally found her voice. "It's good to see you again, Chad. How is it that we always manage to run into each other?"

He smiled, looking at ease. "I'd say you're following me, but I was the one who bumped into you."

She looked at his basket filled with healthy items for several meals. "Looks like you can find your way around the health store now."

Chad chuckled. "Not like the first time I was here."

Lydia laughed. "Not at all. You couldn't have found your hands at the ends of your arms that day."

"Wish I could argue that point. It was good to see you and Dean at the meeting. Things look like they're going better." It sounded more like a question.

"Yeah. We'll see how long that lasts."

"Dean would be stupid to keep ignoring you, Lyds." He cleared his throat. "I mean, Lydia. Sorry, old habits."

"You can call me Lyds."

Chad grabbed a bottle without looking at what it was. "I should get back. Alyssa and I are making dinner together tonight."

Lydia's heart ached. She wished he was making dinner with her. Lydia forced a smile. "Sounds like fun. Tell her I say hi."

He nodded. "Will do." He stepped back.

"Oh, and Chad."

He looked at her, raising an eyebrow. Oh, he was hot…and she really missed him.

She cleared her throat. "I'm really glad you're happy." She meant it, though it hurt her. He deserved to be happy, even if it wasn't with her.

"Thanks, and I'm really glad to see things are getting better for you. No one deserves it more than you. Bye, Lydia."

"Bye," she whispered, watching him walk away. What she wouldn't give to have a heart-to-heart with him. Nothing was better than their talks—except maybe what followed the talks—but those days were over. She grabbed an extra bottle and made her way to the registers.

Lydia set the basket on the conveyor belt, removed the reusable bags from her shoulder, and set them on top. She looked around and saw Chad in the next line over. Lydia looked away, not wanting to think about him anymore.

The line moved quickly, and soon the cashier told Lydia the total. She pulled a credit card from her purse, and handed it to the lady. She ran it through the machine, and then looked confused. She slid it again before handing it to Lydia. "I'm sorry, but it's not working for some reason."

Lydia's cheeks heated with embarrassment. "It should be—it worked earlier. Can you try it again? Third time's a charm." She handed it back. Lydia could feel stares around her.

The cashier ran it again. "Sorry. Maybe it expired or ran out of funds."

Lydia's face burned hotter. "We're not out of money." She dug into her purse for another card, and handed it to the lady.

She slid it through the machine. "Sorry. This one doesn't work, either."

"Well, I'll have to give the bank a call. In the meantime, I'll pay cash for this." Lydia dug in her purse for what cash she had, and then handed it to the lady.

She counted it out, and then said, "You're short twenty-five thirty-three."

"Dammit!" Tears sprang to Lydia's eyes. There was no more money in her purse. She'd have to decide what to leave at the store.

"I've got it."

Lydia looked up to see Chad handing the cashier a fifty. Her cheeks burned all the more. "Thanks, Chad," Lydia mumbled.

"No problem. That's what neighbors are for." He looked into her eyes. "Keep the change. You might need it."

"I'll pay you back. I promise." Lydia held her head high, though she'd never been so humiliated in all her life. Having Chad witness the entire thing—and save the day—only made it worse.

"No worries. Hope you get your bank troubles fixed." He waved, and walked away.

The cashier handed Lydia the change and receipt. She stuffed them into her purse, grabbed her bags, and got out of the store as fast as she could. She was so angry she actually peeled out of the parking lot.

That was her favorite grocery store, and she didn't think she'd ever be able to show her face there again. They would probably put her on a list of some kind, anyway. Losers who couldn't pay probably had to use cash every time. Her face burned even more as she sped through a yellow light.

When she got home, Lydia sat parked in the garage for a few minutes. She was so upset, she shook. Embarrassed tears sprung to her eyes. She had spoken with employees there hundreds of times. In fact, she knew most of them by name. That made the whole thing worse.

And why had Chad needed to witness it? The worst thing about the whole ordeal was the look of pity in his eyes. A tear escaped and ran down her face. She didn't want his pity. It would be better if he hated her than felt sorry for her.

Time ticked away, and Lydia had to get the groceries in the fridge before they spoiled in the hot garage. She reached between the seats and grabbed the bags from the back. Then she got out of the car and slammed the door as hard as she could.

If Dean called before the banks opened in the morning, Lydia would demand to know what had happened. He had so much money it practically spilled from every opening in his body. There was no reason at all for them to deny her cards. Every single one of her cards were good for at least two more years. She'd bought enough stuff online to know that much.

Lydia went inside, slamming that door, too. How would she ever look at Chad again in a meeting? She knew he would never tell anyone about what happened—he was too good a man to do that. But still, *he* knew. Lydia would almost rather have the entire HOA have seen that than just Chad.

The change from his fifty jingled in her purse as she dropped it on the counter. Lydia sat down at the table and let the tears flow. She wasn't really one to cry, but it was all too much. Dean, the credit cards, Chad. What was next?

Gloating

CARA OPENED HER eyes. She had been woken by Dean's laughter, and since her head rested on his warm, bare chest it bounced up and down with each chuckle.

"What's going on?" she asked, her voice sounding groggy.

Dean held up his phone. "Just got some alerts. Lydia tried to use her credit cards, but they've been frozen."

Cara scowled. "You woke me for that?"

He ran his palms over her forehead. "I didn't mean to, baby. Don't you think it's funny?"

"I don't really care. I'd rather sleep."

Dean kissed her cheek, and moved away from her. "I'll go downstairs so you can."

Cara regretted her words. "No, Dean. I'd rather be with you. Don't leave me alone. You travel enough as it is."

Irritation flashed across his face. "I'm so sick of hearing that all the time. Really, I am. You know I have to work to pay for everything."

"What's the deal with Lydia?" Cara asked, sitting up. "I mean, I know what you've told me, but there's no reason to keep her around. It's not like she can give you babies. You're not tied down to her. Just cut her off."

"Spoken like a true friend."

"Dean."

He took a deep breath. "Look, baby. You know I love you. I bought this house so we could be together here, not in my cramped condo. Things will all come together. I promise. I just need to be careful."

"Careful about what? She has nothing, except what you've given her. If you cut her off, she'll have no choice but to run back home to the trailer park she grew up in and be the trash she was always meant to be."

"Don't talk about her like that."

Cara narrowed her eyes. "You still care about her."

"Let's talk about something else."

"No. Do you have feelings for her?"

"So what if I do, Cara? She's my wife."

Cara snorted. "Wife? You haven't slept with her in *years*. I know because she's whined about it more times than I could count. Do you know what it's like being in her circle of friends?" Cara changed her tone to whiny and annoying. "Dean doesn't love me. Dean's having affairs—I just know it. Dean won't touch me. Dean's disgusted by me. Blah, blah, blah. Just punch me in the throat, please."

Dean looked annoyed, but then burst out laughing. "You almost sound just like her." His face turned serious. "Now stop."

"What do you see in that whiny piece of trailer trash?"

"She's not trailer trash."

"Born poor, always poor, Dean. She may love spending your money, but no matter what, she can't get away from her roots. What do you see in her?"

"You really want to know?"

"Yeah. I don't get it."

Dean sighed, looking lost in thought. "She believed in me when no one else did."

Cara scooted closer and ran her fingers over his sculpted chest. "But that was a long time ago. Does she now?"

He put his hand on top of hers, pressing it against his skin. She could feel his heart beating against his chest. Thump, thump, thump. "I think so."

"Really? Even after all your marital troubles? You don't think she's found anyone else, do you?"

Dean's eyebrows came together. "One guy. And really, who could blame her? Besides, she's hot. I'm surprised she's stayed that faithful to me after all the women I've—"

"Yeah, yeah. Okay." Cara scowled. "You really think she's hot?"

"I may not like her much, but I'm not blind."

"You're going to marry me someday, right?"

"Cara." His tone held not only irritation, but warning.

"Seriously. We're going to have a family. A *family*, Dean."

"Would you stop saying my name? I've never met anyone who says my name so much when talking to me."

She scooted away, hurt. "Why are you being so mean? Is it because we're talking about Lydia?"

"I don't even know why you want to talk about her. You always say how much you can't stand her."

"And that's part of why you like me so much, right? Everyone else adores her. You've made her into someone that people actually like."

"People liked her before she met me."

"Why are you defending her?"

"No matter what you say, she's my wife."

"And no matter what happens, I'll always be the mother of your child."

He glared at her.

"Tell me one redeeming quality she has, and I'll drop the subject."

"She's a good cook."

Cara rolled her eyes. "That's all you have? You could hire someone to do that."

"You said you'd drop it."

"And I said name a quality. Cooking is a skill."

"Damn. Women are annoying."

"I'll pretend you didn't say that," Cara said. "What's one good thing about her? Just one."

Dean's face softened. "She can see the best in anyone, even a total jerk. Is that a quality, or still only a skill?"

"Could go either way. Though I haven't heard her say anything good about you." Cara shot him a dirty look.

"I don't know why I put up with either of you."

"At least you have benefits from me," Cara said. She moved to her side, allowing the strap on her shirt to slide down her shoulder.

Dean looked away. Was that guilt on his face?

"You've got to be kidding me," Cara said, sitting up.

"What?" he stared at her.

"Don't tell me you've actually slept with her recently." A sick feeling welled up in her stomach.

"It's none of your business."

Cara's eyes widened. "Dean! How could you?"

"I need a drink. Get some sleep. I don't need two whiny, jealous women to deal with." He climbed out of bed, and put his shirt back on.

Cara's heart pounded. "I'm not whiny... or jealous," she lied. She wanted to dig her fingernails into Lydia's eyes and rip them out of her skull. After all those years, why would Lydia sleep with Dean now?

"I need some space."

The last thing Cara wanted was to be alone, especially since Dean just got back from traveling. She forced herself to smile. "Stay, Dean. I'm sorry. It must be my hormones." She crawled over to his side of the bed as seductively as she could with a bulging belly. Cara grabbed onto his shirt and pulled herself up, pushing herself against him. "You can talk about anything you want. I won't interrupt."

He raised an eyebrow

Cara ran her palm down his arms. "Tell me about how you manage to stay ripped despite working so much." She squeezed his muscles. "You're so strong. Tell me all about it."

Dean's face softened further, and he sat down.

Cara climbed into his lap, running her fingertips along his chest, and down to his perfect six-pack. She tucked her fingers under his shirt and pulled it up over his head. She threw it on the floor. "There. That's better."

He grinned looking more relaxed.

"What do you want to talk about?" she asked in her most sultry voice. "Or what would you rather do?" She would do whatever it took to make him happy so that he would never want to return to his skank of a wife ever again.

Dean's phone played a tune indicating that he had a new text. He picked it up, looked at it, and laughed.

"What's so funny?" Cara asked.

"She tried to use another card. This time online. I'll bet she's frustrated."

Cara's mouth curved upward. "I'll bet. Did you freeze her cards on purpose?"

"Yeah."

"Why?" asked Cara.

"I thought you said you were going to listen to what I said without saying anything."

"Did I? Well, you're not telling me enough."

"She took out a large sum of cash from the bank today. I'm sure doesn't think I know, but I keep tabs on what she does. It helps to have friends in high places."

"I'm sure it does." Clara kissed the soft skin on his shoulder.

He moved his head to the side, inviting her to kiss his neck, which she did. Cara kissed a path up to his ear, and then whispered, "Tell me more."

Dean moaned, and then kissed her on the mouth. "She's sneaking around about something. Bought a computer with some of the cash she took out of the bank. It's going beyond her secretly working for a paper behind my back."

Cara slid her hands down his back. "Oh?"

"I'm not sure what it is, but I fully intend to find out. I always do."

"Always?" she dug her nails into his skin, and he let out a gasp. "Do tell," she whispered in his ear.

He kissed her greedily. "I have my ways."

"Do you know who her guy was?" Cara bit his lip, and then moved her kisses toward his ear, giving him the chance to talk. Not that she cared what he had to say, except to pick up some good gossip.

"Of course I know. It was that Mercer prick from the HOA. He thinks he's such a hotshot because of his blog."

"You don't care?" She nibbled on his earlobe.

"Nah. It kept her off my back about not paying any attention to her. Oh...," he moaned. "She was actually pleasant to live with until they split up. I sent a large anonymous donation to the reward for his missing kid as a thanks for distracting Lydia."

Pieces

"**W**ANT US TO help clean the mess?" Bri asked Lydia as they got up from the table on the porch.

"I can get it," Lydia said, trying to be the good hostess. Deep down, she wanted the help, or at least for them to stick around longer. It had felt so good to play card games and gossip. She hadn't had to think about any of her problems for a solid three hours.

Savannah gave Lydia an apologetic look. "I'm sorry, Lyds. I gotta get back home. Tom's probably already back from his poker game. It's a day that ends in a 'y,' so you know what that means." She winked.

"Savannah," Bri exclaimed. "Have some courtesy. Lyds isn't getting anything from anyone."

"Really?" Savannah raised an eyebrow. "I saw the way Dean looked at her at the HOA meeting. You two got it on right before the meeting, am I correct?"

Lydia looked away. "And after."

Bri gasped. "Seriously? You didn't tell us?"

"I'm sure it's nothing. He probably just had a spat with whatever tramp he's seeing this month."

Savannah kissed Lydia's cheek. "Take advantage of it while you can. You always used to brag about…his skills."

"Goodnight, Savannah." Lydia shook her head.

"Nightie-night." Savannah kissed Bri's cheek, and then headed inside, toward the front door. "Meet you ladies at the mall tomorrow?" she called.

"Wouldn't miss it," Bri hollered.

"Maybe," Lydia said, grabbing the empty wine glasses.

Bri grabbed Lydia's arms. "You and Dean seriously…?"

Lydia shrugged. "Probably nothing."

"Once could be nothing. Twice is something, sweetie."

"It's called horny." Lydia carried the glasses into the kitchen.

"Why do I get the feeling you're keeping something from me?" Bri set the snack dishes, all piled on top of each other, on the counter. "What is it?"

Lydia rinsed out the glasses. "He left a rose on the bed before catching his plane."

Bri's already large eyes widened. "Shut up."

"It was from out front, but still."

Bri leaned against the island. "Do you think he's having a change of heart?"

Lydia shrugged. "Maybe." But even if he was, did it matter? He was serial killer. Not just *Oops, I accidentally killed someone*, but *I've killed more than a handful of times, and am proud enough of it to keep evidence.*

"What aren't you telling me?"

"Everyone has secrets, Bri. He has his, and his recent kindness has nothing to do with how he feels about me."

"Secrets? You know about his affairs, and you've never cared."

"Never cared? Really, Bri?"

"Fine. But you haven't cared since Chad." Bri raised an eyebrow, and then went back out to the deck and came back with more plates. She set them down, and then put her arm around Lydia's shoulders. "Are you really okay? All night you've seemed… I can't really put my finger on it, but I would have to say spooked."

Lydia jumped back. "Really? Why would I be?"

"Sweetie, you tell me. You haven't been yourself since…." Bri looked up and twisted her pretty face. "That evening you made a mess and didn't show up for our girls' night out."

Sighing, Lydia stared at her best friend. She really wanted to tell her about her suspicions, but Bri would really flip out. She would probably never sleep again. She hadn't slept for days after a home invasion next door to her. This was a lot worse.

"Well, whenever you're ready to talk, you know my number."

Lydia hugged Bri. "Thank you, Bri. I love you."

"Me too, sweetie." Her phone beeped. She looked at it. "Will you be okay if I go? Looks like Corey's back from the boys' poker game."

"Go. You know I'm used to having this huge house to myself."

"Oh, sweetie." Bri's puppy-dog eyes were full of pity.

Lydia cleared her throat. "Don't look at me like that, or I'll have to smack you."

Bri laughed. "That's better. Call me in the morning. 'Kay?"

"Sure, no problem."

Bri grabbed her purse from the counter. "See ya, sweetie."

"You too." Lydia waved, and then went outside to see what was left on the table. Just the deck of cards and some organic-candy wrappers. She went over to the railing and leaned against it, looking up at the stars.

It was hard to believe it was the same night sky she had looked up at as a kid with her brother. They used to discuss how enormous the universe was. When put into perspective, her life and her problems didn't seem so important. The entire planet was just a speck of dust in the vast greatness of everything.

She continued to stare until a shooting star came into view. When its light died, Lydia realized how tired she was. She grabbed the rest of the wrappers from the table and carried them inside, closing the sliding glass door behind her and locking it.

Lydia dumped the stuff on the counter, too tired to clean it up then. She'd just take care of it in the morning. It wasn't like Dean was going to be home before then, anyway.

She forced herself up the stairs after checking the doors and setting the alarm, and barely got herself ready for bed before climbing in and falling asleep as she hit the pillow. Stressful dreams plagued her all night, and when she woke up with the sun shining on her, Lydia barely felt more rested.

Her mind raced. She needed to look into the credit cards before Dean found out. He would be pissed that they couldn't access their money. He worked hard for it, and never appreciated anyone keeping it from him.

Lydia worried that her trip the day before had been a bad idea. What if Angie was able to find her, and came asking questions? There was no way Lydia could explain that to Dean.

Her stomach twisted in tight knots, making her feel sick. She was probably better off just leaving, but what she needed was to start stashing cash—or was there time for it? He was supposed to be back sometime this week, but then he probably would be gone all month after that.

Why hadn't she been collecting money since long ago? Starting when their marriage began to sour. That should have been her clue to do something to take care of herself. But at first, she had convinced herself that things could be saved. Then she was so upset to realize they probably wouldn't... and then she thought she and Chad would end up together. Not only would he be able to take care of her financially, but she'd have been able to work if she wanted.

Chad had always said that if that was what she wanted, she should go for it. He even encouraged her to go after her dreams while she was still with Dean. She obviously had done that, but she'd had all funds sent to her family since they needed it so badly, and also, she hadn't wanted Dean questioning where the extra money came from.

She felt more trapped than ever. Why had she stayed with him? Just so she could have nice things? It had made sense at the time, but now it seemed like the stupidest decision anyone could make.

If the news clippings were any indicator of when he started his spree, Lydia could have easily left long before then. Or would she have been his first victim? She shuddered at the thought, and then pulled up the blankets to her neck despite the house already being warm. The AC would kick on later, after it really warmed up.

The worst part was having no one to tell. She *had* to tell someone. Whether it was Chad, Bri, or her brother, she couldn't keep doing this on her own. Chad or her brother would probably be the best choices, because they would both be able to keep a level head. Bri was a great friend, but Lydia just didn't think she could handle something like that.

What about Cara or Savannah? Not Cara. She was hormonal and emotional as it was, and Lydia couldn't shake the feeling that she was angry at her for something. Savannah was easily the toughest of the bunch, though Lydia was a close second.

So, it was between her brother, Chad, and Savannah. Lydia would think about it as she got ready. She climbed into the shower and let the hot water massage her as she tried to forget her troubles for a while. She stayed in until the water went cold, and then she got ready for the day.

Once out of the shower and dressed, Lydia felt like a caged animal in the house. Who knew what Dean was doing right then? Could he be killing some poor girl at that very moment? If so, that was on her—at least in part. She was keeping quiet when she needed to tell someone. The cops, in particular.

She took a deep breath. There were reasons she couldn't go to them yet. They'd laugh her out of the station based on what she had, and then Dean would probably find out... and that could *not* happen.

Lydia put on some mascara and lipstick and went for a drive. It felt good to be out of the house, but she was too on edge to keep sitting. She found a high school with a nice-looking track to walk around.

The night air was nice and the quiet helped her to think as she walked around and around. After a while, she was aware of someone else going around the track. She paid enough attention to him to be safe, but not enough to look at him. She had to figure everything out.

"Lydia?"

Her heart stopped and she turned to look at the man. He wore tight-fitting exercise pants, bright tennis shoes, and a hoodie with a horse on it. She stared at his face, trying to figure out where she'd seen him before.

"Toby. We met at my sister's HOA meeting."

Lydia stopped walking and tried to remember. Then in her mind, she saw a cowboy hat covering much of his face. "Dakota's brother. You have the horse."

"Flash, my prize-winning beauty."

"Right. How's life on the farm?"

"Ranch." Toby grabbed a shoe and stretched his leg.

"You don't look much like a rancher," Lydia said.

"I don't always wear a cowboy hat. It's not very practical most of the time, but I do enjoy wearing one when I can."

Lydia smiled. "I'm not usually a fan of them, but you made it work."

He grinned. "I bet you'd look good in one. You could always come over to the ranch sometime and check out my horses."

She relaxed and looked him over. Horses weren't the only thing she was interested in checking out. "That sounds like fun," she said, pulling out her phone. "What's your number?"

He told her and then she put it in her phone and then called his cell. Toby pulled it out and looked at it.

Lydia held up her phone. "Now you have my number, too."

"Perfect. It was great running into you, Lydia. I've got to get back and feed the horses. But we'll be in touch soon. Okay?"

"I'd like that. Bye, Toby."

He ran off, waving, and then Lydia went back to her car. She thought about Toby the whole way back home.

When she got into her bedroom, Lydia noticed the light blinking on her phone. Her heart sank. Who could that be? She walked over to the bed and checked. She had a text from her boss wanting to know when her column would be ready. She threw the phone down. Had she missed her deadline already?

If she was going to leave Dean, she really couldn't afford to screw that up. She would have to prove that she could handle it, and more. She needed what little it provided, and probably an additional column. Maybe more than that. If she stayed with her family, she could save up then.

Oh, there was just too much to think about. Her life was falling to pieces right before her eyes. When had everything gotten so complicated? And when would it all go back to what it used to be? And what life, exactly, did she want back? When she was happy with her serial-killer husband? When she was happy with someone else's husband?

She picked up the phone and texted her boss that it was coming soon. Lydia looked at the time. She could probably get something ready and send it within the hour. It wouldn't be her best work, but it would do.

Encounter

L YDIA CLOSED HER laptop and looked at the time. It had taken her less than an hour to read the questions, write out the responses, and run them through a quick editing program. At least the questions had been easy enough to answer. They were so basic, part of her wanted to reach out through the computer and slap the askers.

They should be glad their problems were so easily solved. One girl wrote that she thought her boyfriend was seeing her best friend. *Walk away from them both, stupid!* But of course, Lydia hadn't said that. She— no Layla—had told her make sure she was certain before confronting them. Then she told her in the nicest way possible to get new friends.

Another girl was in love with her college professor. That was an easy one to answer. It had to do with putting his job on the line, so Lydia had to give a good moral answer. If you really care about him, don't put him in a situation that would probably get him fired.

Where was the advice column for wives of serial killers? Lydia froze. Everything was online. There had to be some kind of group. She could create another fake online person, or even use the same one. Ashley would work, and it was already set up.

But if she was going to do that, she needed to take the new laptop somewhere out of town again. First, she would grab some breakfast, and then head for a new coffee shop.

If she could find others who had been through the same thing, they could offer clarity that she lacked. Lydia knew that acting from a place of fear wasn't in her best interest. She would make poor decisions. When people were scared, they never thought things through, and it was nearly impossible to see a situation for what it was.

Lydia couldn't afford to make mistakes. One wrong move, and Dean could find out that she knew his secret. He would have no problem killing her. It would probably just be another day for him, except that he wouldn't be able to just walk away like with the others. There was no evidence linking him to them, except that he'd been in the same areas for work at the same time.

Without any real detective work, she wouldn't find any proof of him having spent time with any of the victims. Talking with Angie had proven that. Dean probably swooped in, wooed them into dates, and then went in for the kill—in the most literal way possible.

Even if he had left some trace or trail, he had surely cleaned it up. From what she'd read in all the clippings, the police had nothing to go on, and they all thought the killings were random. Even if they were to compare them all, they wouldn't think it was the same person. Dean had done away with each one differently.

Unless it really wasn't him. Could he be hiding the clues for someone else? Covering the tracks for a friend or colleague? Maybe there was someone who traveled with him that he hadn't mentioned. It wasn't like he ever told Lydia any details about his work life. Or what if he was trying to solve these cases himself?

Was she trying to protect him or trying to convince herself that she hadn't been stupid enough to marry a psychopath? Wouldn't she have seen the signs?

She really needed to find an online group and figure out how to get to the bottom of this. She was going to go crazy if she didn't. If only she could ask Dean about the clippings…but she couldn't accuse someone of murder without more proof than that, and it wasn't like she could travel around the country, chasing down relatives of the deceased.

Not only would she likely end up as empty-handed as the day before, but she couldn't get away with traveling to the other locations without Dean knowing. That's why she had to get to a nearby town and find out what she could online. It was time to get aggressive friending anyone who had anything to do with anyone in the clippings.

After eating, she got a text from Bri. *Still on for the mall this morning?*

Lydia groaned. She had completely forgotten about their plans. Maybe she could swing by for a little bit. She definitely need to relax. Lydia started writing a response when she heard the garage door.

Dean was back already? She hadn't even had a chance to look into the credit card issues yet.

She deleted her text and sent Bri a message saying Dean just got home.

So are you joining us?

Her heart pounded. It would be the perfect excuse to get away. The last thing she needed was for him to realize that anything was wrong and start asking questions. Usually, she could lie about anything like a pro. It had started when she would sneak out of the house in high school, and she had been so good at it that she practiced the art as often as possible for years. But she was so shaken by Dean's clippings, Lydia wasn't sure she could keep her cool.

Well?

Lydia heard Dean's car door slam shut.

I don't know. I need to talk to him first.

Don't ditch us again. A little, animated pouty face followed the words.

I'll try not to, but I should talk to him since he's home.

Yeah, I know. Let me know when you're on your way.

Sure.

If you're not here soon, I'll assume you got lucky. Two animated faces kissed each other.

Lydia shook her head. *You do that.* She slid the phone into her pocket as the door to the garage opened, and she heard Dean's footsteps headed her way.

"Morning," he said.

She nodded. "Rough flight?"

"Something like that. I barely slept."

He looked so tired and stressed, the part of her that still loved him couldn't help feeling bad for him. Lydia knew she should ignore it, but after reconnecting with him, that side of her had been awakened. "Do you need anything? I can fry up some bacon. I think we have enough eggs for omelets. I know how much you love those."

Dean ran his hands through his hair. "You'd do that?"

"You look like you could use some nourishment."

"That would be great. I smell like the plane. Let me shower while you get that ready."

She'd used all the hot water. He would be pissed. "Do you want anything special in your eggs?"

"Surprise me." He headed for the stairs.

Lydia pulled out her phone and sent Bri a text saying she was going to have breakfast with Dean.

Bri sent back a string of animated kissing faces.

By the time Dean came downstairs, Lydia had the table set and the food ready. Dean sat at his regular spot, and Lydia set a plate in front of him. Instead of sitting in her normal spot, she sat next to him on his left.

"This smells delicious. Are those onions?"

Lydia nodded, hoping he still liked those.

"Mmm. My favorite." Dean leaned over and kissed her. He smelled of her favorite aftershave. Lydia's heart skipped a beat. He still had that?

She rubbed his smooth face, taking in more of the scent. "You smell so good."

He smiled at her, his eyes still looking tired. The lines around them appeared deeper than usual. Not that she had paid much attention to them in recent years.

"Thanks for making the food." He kissed her again, and then dug in. He placed his left hand on her knee and squeezed.

Lydia's eyes widened, still not used to his renewed interest in her. She relaxed, and then ate her small omelet. She'd already had some cereal before he'd arrived. As she ate, she couldn't take her mind off his hand resting on her knee.

She watched him as he ate. His focus was on the meal, so he didn't even notice her looking his way. She studied his face, finding that he looked not only tired, but stressed as well.

When he had emptied the plate, he wiped his mouth with a napkin, and looked over at her. "Those are even better than I remember. I don't know what I did to deserve your recent cooking, but I'm glad I did it." He smiled, and then squeezed her knee again.

Lydia shrugged. "You just seemed stressed. I should let you get some sleep."

His hand inched up her leg. "Or you could join me."

She stared into his eyes, her pulse racing. Instead of seeing the man she had hated for so long, she saw the man she had fallen in love with—the one who had once cared deeply for her. Lydia nodded, unable to find her voice.

Dean took her hand and led her up to their room. He looked at her. "You forgot to make the bed."

"I didn't mean to. My—"

"It's perfect, Lyds." He wrapped his arms around her, pulling her close.

Conflicted

LYDIA WATCHED DEAN sleep. He didn't snore like usual. Butterflies danced in her stomach thinking about possibly having her marriage return to what it had once been. Could things really be in the process of turning around?

Guilt tugged at her for snooping behind his back. Maybe she just needed to trust him. He'd never given her or anyone else a reason to think he was killing anyone.

But what if he was killing people? She was the only one who suspected anything, and if she could do anything to prevent it from happening again, she needed to. There was no way she could live with herself if she didn't.

"Dean, what are you hiding from me?" she whispered.

He stirred and she jumped, but he didn't wake.

"Won't you tell me your secret?" she asked.

Dean's eyes fluttered open. Lydia's heart jumped into her throat.

He grabbed her hand. "Don't let me keep you from your plans for the day," he said, his voice groggy. "I just need some sleep." He kissed her palm, the softness of the touch tickling her skin.

"Sweet dreams." She leaned over and kissed his forehead. His eyes closed, and almost immediately, his breathing deepened. She got out of bed and slid her clothes back on. One look in the mirror told her that her hair was a disaster. She didn't have time for another shower, so she just twisted it into a bun and tied it up.

When she got downstairs, she cleaned the kitchen. It was a mess not only from breakfast, but the night before with the girls. She threw all the dishes in the washer and gave the counters and table a quick wipe. That would have to do.

Lydia grabbed her purse and then went to her car. She opened the garage door and then turned the key in the ignition. Tears welled up in her eyes. Why did everything have to be so complicated?

It had been so long since Dean had paid her any attention, and she had to find the clippings now, of all times? If only she knew who to talk to. The more she thought about it, the less convinced she was that anyone in her life would make a good confidant.

Her phone buzzed, and she pulled it out of her pocket sure it was Bri again.

Should we expect you or not? We're trying to decide whether to stay or hit a movie.

I'm on my way.

Yay. We'll stay.

Lydia took a deep breath, and then checked her makeup. Her tears hadn't ruined it, at least. She backed up, and headed for the mall. It was close to lunch time, and the parking lot was pretty full. She was going to have to park near the back.

Lydia checked the trunk, making sure her laptop was still hidden. She couldn't take any risks that anyone would see it if she had to open the trunk. Once she was sure it just looked like a normal trunk, she made the trek to the entrance. It took her a minute to spot her friends—they stood by the fountain where they usually met. It looked like only Bri and Savannah had made it. Cara had been so moody lately, it was somewhat of a relief to not have to deal with her.

While she was still a ways away, Bri and Savannah waved to her. Lydia waved back and picked up her speed, darting around kids running around, chasing each other.

"Did someone have a good morning?" asked Savannah in a sing-song voice.

"So, Dean's finally figured out what a good thing he has," Bri said. "Maybe we can all hang out again. It was fun when we hung out with the guys, too."

"I've always said not to let me stop you."

"We haven't," Savannah said, "but it would be a lot more fun to have you and Dean join us."

"Where's Cara?" Lydia asked.

"I haven't heard from her in a couple days," Bri said. "She's not answering calls or texts."

"You think she has post-partum depression?" asked Lydia.

"That's after the baby's born," Bri said, rolling her eyes.

Lydia narrowed her eyes. "And how would I know that?"

"Even I knew that," Savannah said, "and I don't have kids, either."

"Maybe we should stop by the house and drag her out," Lydia said. "From what she said before, Ethan finds her gross. She might just need an intervention."

"You know," Bri said, her bright eyes widening, "that's a fantastic idea. Who's up for a trip to the spa? Cara would love that."

"I could use some pampering," Lydia said, smiling. But then she remembered the credit cards, and her severe lack of cash. "But I think I left my wallet at home."

"No worries," Savannah said. "I owe you from dinner a few weeks ago, remember?"

Relief flooded Lydia. "That works."

Less than twenty minutes later, they all pulled up in front of the Ross house.

"Her car isn't there," Lydia pointed out. "Just Ethan's."

"Probably in the garage," Bri said, flipping some hair behind her shoulder. "Let's go."

"Doesn't Ethan keep the garage full of crap that annoys Cara?" Lydia asked, but her two friends were already walking toward the front door.

Lydia caught up just as Savannah rang the doorbell.

Ethan opened the door, looking annoyed. "Didn't Cara tell you guys that she doesn't live here anymore?"

All three of them gasped, and asked surprised questions.

"I don't know where she is, and frankly, I don't care."

"But she's carrying your baby," Lydia said. "Don't you care about that?"

Ethan gave her a disgusted look. "It's not my baby."

"What?" Lydia asked. Was that why Cara had been acting strange lately? She looked over at Bri and Savannah, noticing that neither of them appeared as shocked by the news as she did.

"She hasn't returned our calls," Bri said. "You don't have any idea where she would have gone?"

"Try asking her boyfriend." Ethan closed the door.

"Did you two already know?" Lydia asked. "You don't seem surprised that it's not his."

Savannah gave her a saddened look. "Well, you haven't been around as much over the last week, and yeah, she told us."

"You guys didn't think to clue me in? I feel like everyone is hiding things from me."

They both looked uncomfortable. Bri spoke up. "Sweetie, I thought—"

"Don't 'sweetie' me, Bri." Lydia glared at her best friend.

Bri frowned. "We just thought it was something she should probably tell you herself."

"Why? Is there more to the story than you're telling me?"

Savannah and Bri exchanged a look.

Anger boiled up in Lydia's chest. "Fine. I have things I need to do today, anyway. If you figure out where Cara is, don't bother telling me. I'll find a way to figure it out myself."

"Lyds," Bri said.

"Wait," Savannah said, pleading with her eyes.

"Catch you later." Lydia turned around and stormed to her car. Who could she trust? Not even her best friends. For whatever reason, they didn't think they could trust Lydia with Cara's issues. They were all so close. If some of them knew something about Lydia that one of the others didn't, they would've told the one the outs. It just wasn't right.

Everything was changing. Not just her marriage, but her closest friends, too. She unlocked her car, slammed the door, and for the second time in as many days, peeled away. Could she trust anyone?

The only one treating her well was Dean, and he was the one person she really should trust least. He only started to be nice to her when she had given him back the news clipping he had dropped.

That was it.

He wasn't falling back in love with her. Dean was just buttering her up so she wouldn't suspect what she already knew. It was all a show to cover his butt. Fury built up.

Lydia's entire life was a hoax. Her friends didn't trust her, and her husband only pretended to like her. In his fake shows of affection, he probably watched her like a hawk, looking for any small sign of her distrust. Dean was just waiting for her to figure it out.

And she was dumb enough to fall for him each time. She'd fallen for him hard when they first met, and he knew exactly how turn the charm back on, wrapping her around his little finger.

Obviously, he didn't know that she knew—or did he? Was he going to win back her love and trust just in time to get rid of her and any evidence she had? Or was it less sinister? He could be buttering her up just to keep her happy, so she wouldn't find out his secret.

It didn't matter either way, because his affections were all a lie. It was all about him, and nothing to do with his love suddenly being rekindled.

She pulled into a Park and Ride lot, and then parked in a shady spot away from the bus stops. What was she supposed to do now? Pretend to be oblivious to Dean's woos? Wait until he left again, and then pack what she could and disappear?

Where to? Her family? That would be the first place he would look for her.

Someone knocked on her window, and Lydia jumped. She looked up to see Bri and Savannah.

"Go away."

Savannah motioned for her to roll down her window.

Lydia shook her head, and pulled out her phone, pretending to make a call.

Both of her friends motioned for her window to go down. Lydia looked away, talking into her phone. Savannah and Bri moved to the front of her car and waved their arms back and forth.

Lydia waved them away. They shouted her name, and others around stared at them.

"Fine, you win." She shoved her phone in her purse, and then opened the door. "Can't you guys take a hint? I'm pissed, and don't want to talk to either one of you."

They ran over and wrapped their arms around her. "But we love you,"

Bri said.

"Then why keep things from me? I wouldn't do that to you—and you know it."

"Can we sit down?" Bri asked.

Lydia pointed to her car. "Have a seat."

Savannah pointed to some benches not too far away. "How about over there?"

"Are you afraid I'll freak out?" Lydia scowled.

"Maybe," Bri said. The corners of her mouth twitched. "Sweetie, you know we love you. We need to talk."

Lydia gave them both an exasperated look. "This better be good." She would hear them out, and then go. She just needed to get away from everything.

Secrets

B RI WATCHED LYDIA as they walked over to the bench. Every move she made showed Bri that her best friend was stressed out. She'd been acting strange for a while, but if she knew anything about Cara, she wasn't letting on. Something was definitely going on, but it was probably something else.

They reached the bench, and Lydia sat, crossing her arms and her legs.

Bri sat down, carefully considering her words. "Sweetie, we just want everything to be okay with you."

Lydia raised an eyebrow. "That hasn't been the case for a long time."

Savannah sat on the other side of Lydia. "Even so, usually, you walk around with a smile on your face. You're so confident, you make others jealous. But that's faded. Talk to us."

"You're right. Nothing's okay, but I can't bring you guys into it. It wouldn't be fair."

"We're your friends," Bri reminded her. "No matter what."

Lydia looked conflicted. "That's just it. This is bigger than that, and it wouldn't be fair of me to bring you in."

Bri studied her, trying to figure out what was going on. "Look, rain or shine, we're here for you. You kill someone, we're here to find you a place to hide."

Lydia flinched. Bri looked over at Savannah, who gave her a curious look. Bri had struck a nerve somehow.

"It's not like that," Lydia said.

"Obviously," Bri said, forcing a wide smile. "You'd never kill anyone. The point is, we're here for you, and even if you did, we'd find a way to hide the body. We're your girls." Bri put her arm around Lydia and gave a squeeze.

"Really?" Lydia asked, her eyes narrowing. "Friends? Is that why it feels like everyone is hiding something from me?"

Bri and Savannah exchanged another look. She seemed to want Bri's permission to tell what they knew about Cara. Bri shook her head, eyes wide. She couldn't risk Cara spilling her secret. Of course, they'd have to find her for Cara to learn that they'd told Lydia. But given Lydia's recent closeness with Dean, she would likely freak out.

Bri shook her head, eyes focused on Savannah. Bri put her hand on Lydia's arm. "You're right about one thing. Cara has dirt on all of us, and she won't hesitate to use it when she wants to."

Lydia gave her a look that was a cross between exasperated, hurt, and angry. "So, you dragged me out here to let me know you won't tell me what's going on. Thanks."

"It's not like that," Savannah said. "I don't know what Cara's holding over Bri, but I could go to jail if she goes to the cops with what she knows. I'm not sure she wouldn't."

Lydia scowled. "Some friend we have."

Bri's pulse picked up. She didn't even want to admit to her friends what Cara held over her, but at the same time, she couldn't keep the secret from Lydia. If she was falling for Dean again, she had to know what he and Cara had done.

"What we need," Savannah said, "is to find Cara so she can tell you what's going on herself."

"This whole thing is ridiculous." Lydia put her face in her palms, and then looked up. "We used to be so tight. Now we're falling apart. What happened?"

Savannah frowned. "Too much."

"What did you do?" Lydia asked. "You know we're not going to go to the cops with anything."

"I'm sure you won't." Savannah picked at a nail, looking insecure. Bri wasn't sure she'd ever seen Savannah like that. She looked up from the nail, and then made eye contact with both Lydia and Bri. "You know what? Lydia, you're exactly right. Cara only knows because she saw me, and she made sure to hold it over me until she needed me to stay quiet."

Bri's heart pounded so hard it sounded like it was in her ears. Her two friends looked at her expectantly. Bri's stomach lurched. Why had she ever told Cara what she'd done? "Corey would never forgive me if he found out." Bri took a deep breath, trying to calm her nerves. "I can't risk it. Not him."

They all sat in silence for a while, the sun beating down. Were her friends plagued with the same guilt that ran through Bri? She hated thinking about what had happened. It was one stupid mistake, made when she was furious and drunk.

"How long do we have to sit here?" Lydia asked. "I've got to get out of the sun soon."

"Let's go over to the bench over there," Savannah pointed over to the left. "It's in the shade."

They made their way over without a word. Bri's heartbeat had yet to return to normal. She didn't want to admit what had happened with Corey's brother that one awful night. It had been a mistake—a horrible, horrible mistake. He acted like nothing was wrong, but they had both betrayed someone they loved.

Bri couldn't even look at him without remembering that night. Corey never suspected a thing, and for that, Bri was grateful, but she wasn't sure the guilt would ever go away. She feared losing Corey too much to even considering coming clean. Risking him walking away was not something she could deal with.

They were meant to be together, and everyone made mistakes. His brother was hers, and she would have to live with that rest of her life. It had actually served to help their marriage in the long run. Bri always overcompensated for the guilt by treating Corey like a king, which had eventually led to him treating her like a queen.

Before long, they went from a normal, bickering marriage to one everyone pined for. She loved being part of the Bri and Corey Stevens duo that everyone adored and envied.

"Well," Lydia said, starting to stand, "if we're not going to talk, I've got things to do."

"Wait," Savannah said. "Sit back down. I'll talk."

Bri's eyes widened. If Savannah told Lydia about Cara, then Bri's secret was dangerously close to being used by Cara. For all they knew, she was hiding out, spying on them.

Lydia sat, looking at Savannah.

Savannah's face grew serious, and finally tears filled her eyes. "One night, when Tom and I had a really bad fight, I..." She took a deep breath. "I got in the car and drove. I wasn't paying attention to what I was doing, and I, I...." The tears spilled onto her cheeks. "I hit someone. They were jaywalking, and it was just like the movies. The guy flew up onto the hood of the car. He rolled off." Savannah's voice shook. "People came out from a bar, and I freaked out. I was afraid of going to jail, so I drove away." She looked up at the sky. "I don't even know if he lived or not."

"Oh, Savannah." Lydia put her arm around Savannah. "You've been carrying that around?"

"I'm scum."

"No, you're not." Lydia sat taller. "It was an accident, and he shouldn't have been jaywalking."

"It was also dark, and he was wearing all black."

Bri nodded, feeling better about herself. At least she hadn't killed anyone. She wasn't sure how Savannah dealt with that kind of guilt. Bri reached over Lydia and squeezed Savannah's arm. "It doesn't sound like it was your fault."

"But I ran. I could go to jail for that fact alone."

"Wait," Lydia said. "Was that when you said you hit a deer?"

Savannah frowned, and then nodded.

"You've been dealing with that since then?" Lydia exclaimed.

"Cara's evil for holding that against you," Bri said. "How dare she?"

"What's she got against you?" Savannah asked, wiping her eyes.

Bri's stomach twisted in knots. She looked away from her friends and stared at a leaf sitting on the bench. Bri picked it up and played with it. "One night—just one—when I'd had too much drink, and Corey and I weren't getting along...his brother, well, he..." Tears filled her eyes. "If I could take it back, I would. Corey would just die. He loves and trusts the two of us more than anyone else."

She looked over at her two friends. Both of them were wide-eyed.

"I always thought you two had the perfect marriage," Lydia whispered.

"There is no perfect marriage," Savannah said.

They all sat in silence for a few minutes before Lydia spoke up. "Look, I don't want you two to suffer more than you already have. Savannah, I don't want you to go to jail. Bri, you deserve your wonderful marriage with Corey. I don't want either of you to tell me Cara's secret. She'll tell me if she wants me to know. I'm sorry I didn't trust you guys."

Bri squeezed Lydia's hand. "You have nothing to apologize for."

"I feel closer to you guys," Lydia said, "but I'm still not sure about telling you what's bothering me. It's a horrible burden, and I don't want you guys to have to deal with it. Especially not with everything else."

"It's your burden, not ours," Savannah said, taking Lydia's other hand. "We can help you carry it, but it'll crush you if you keep it to yourself. If anyone knows about that, it's me."

"And me," Bri chimed in.

Lydia didn't look convinced.

"Let us support you, sweetie," Bri said. "You've always been there for us."

"But this is huge, and it's not something you'll be able to forget."

"Worse than killing someone?" asked Savannah.

Lydia shook her head. "You know what? I remember hearing about a hit and run a couple towns over around the time you said you hit a deer. He walked away with a broken arm, and if I remember correctly, the police had been looking for him. You may have even done a good deed since he was arrested that night."

Savannah's eyes widened. "Really?"

Lydia nodded, though Bri had her doubts about the validity of Lydia's story. "Just tell us, sweetie." Bri smiled, encouraging her to talk.

They sat in silence again, and then Lydia cleared her throat. "This is huge, and you can't tell anyone—not even Corey or Tom."

"Obviously, I can keep a secret from Corey." Bri frowned.

"Me, too," Savannah said. "You know, from Tom."

Lydia took a deep breath. "I have reason to believe…." She shook her head. "I can't even say it. It's too crazy."

"What is it?" Bri asked in her most soothing voice. She had perfected it with her daughters. "Our lives are full of crazy. Plenty of it."

Her friend shook next to her. Bri wrapped an arm around Lydia. "You can tell us anything."

Savannah nodded in agreement.

"I think Dean's been killing people."

Bri felt like she'd been hit. That had been the last thing she expected Lydia to say. She'd known it had to have been worse than the affairs. They had already known about those long enough.

Savannah made eye contact with Bri.

Cara.

She was probably with Dean, and she carried his baby. If he was going to kill anyone, Cara and her smart mouth would be first on his list.

"Someone say something," Lydia said in a small voice.

"How do you know?" Savannah asked.

"I found some news clippings he's been hiding. The dates and places match up with his work travels." She went into more detail about them. "Why else would he keep them?"

"And he started…being nice to you after he knew you saw one?" Savannah asked.

Lydia nodded.

"Do you think he's killing women he he's having affairs with?" asked Bri. If Cara was in danger, they would have to tell Lydia everything.

Relief

LYDIA LOOKED BACK and forth between her two friends, trying to figure out if they really believed her or not. They both looked horrified, but they didn't seem to doubt what she said.

"Lydia?" asked Bri.

"I don't think he had relationships with the women he killed. He's not a suspect, and in most cases, the victims' friends and family didn't think they had been involved with anyone. None of them, from what I can gather, even were supposed to have had a date that night. I think he probably met them, took them out on a whim—or at least what seemed that way to the girls—and then he… he killed them."

"You don't think there could be another explanation?" Savannah asked.

Lydia shook her head. "I've tried to come up with anything else, but that's the only explanation. Why would he save—and hide—the clippings? Why would he act so suspicious when I gave him the one he was careless enough to drop?"

They all sat in silence.

"You believe me, right?" Lydia asked.

"Of course, sweetie," Bri said, looking distressed.

"We know you wouldn't lie about something like this," Savannah said.

"Do you think I'm jumping to conclusions? I *want* to believe that I'm wrong—that there's some other explanation—but what else is there? Am I missing something?"

Savannah took Lydia's hand. "My head is spinning. This is literally the craziest and scariest thing I've ever heard. Based on what you've told us, I think you need to get out of that house today. Ask questions later."

"I couldn't agree more," Bri said, taking Lydia's other hand. "Stay in our guest room, please. I'll lie to Dean's face if he asks."

"And put your kids in danger?" Lydia asked. "No. I won't."

"Then come to my house," Savannah said. "You know Tom could beat the crap out of Dean—and he'd do it in a heartbeat, too."

Lydia shook her head. "I don't want to put either of you at risk. That's why I didn't want to say anything in the first place."

"Well, we're involved now," Savannah said. "And I don't want you alone with him."

"I appreciate it, but if he was going to hurt me, don't you think he would have done so already?" Lydia asked.

Savannah and Bri exchanged a look.

"Are you afraid he's going to go after you?" Bri asked, her eyes wide.

"I don't think so." Lydia squirmed, hating the question.

"You don't *think* so?" Savannah asked. "How can you stay in that house? In the same bed?"

"If I act weird, he's going to know that I suspect something. For now, he buys my dumb act. He really thinks I believe he dropped an ad he cut out."

Savannah grabbed her arm. "But what if he figures out that you've seen his stash? Then what?"

Lydia's heart raced even faster. "I...I don't know. I can't think. It's all too terrifying."

Bri grabbed her hand. "You've got to get out of there."

"You have to go to the cops," Savannah said.

"With what?" Lydia asked. "I don't have any proof. The cops working all those cases don't have anything. If it is him, he hasn't left behind a single strand of DNA or a fingerprint. His trips are circumstantial at best. With nothing else to go on, he'll know I spilled the beans, and then I'll be his next victim."

"You can't live in fear like this, Lyds," Bri said. "And if he is guilty, he needs to be stopped. He could do it again."

"I realize that," she snapped. "But I'm stuck. Don't you get that? I need to find more than just the clippings. I've actually done some digging, but I can't find anything. He's covered his tracks well."

"He's good at that," Bri muttered.

"Bri," exclaimed Savannah.

"What do you mean?" Lydia asked.

"His affairs, Lyds. Do you have even the slightest inclination as to who even one is?" Bri raised an eyebrow.

Lydia frowned. "No." After having Dean back to acting like he loved her, no matter how fake it was, made the thought of his affairs hurt again. "I wish you girls would tell me that I'm insane for thinking he's actually killing those women."

"Me, too, sweetie." Bri squeezed her hand. "Me too."

"You really don't think that's enough evidence to take to the police?" Savannah asked. "I mean, seriously. They have the manpower to look into this. None of us have any detective training."

"What if they don't believe me?" Lydia asked, shaking. "If they question him, he'll know I'm the one who turned him in. The only reason he's being nice is because he knows there's a chance I saw that one clipping. I can't even imagine what he would do if he knew I'd seen them all." Tears filled her eyes.

Savannah looked into her eyes. "You need to make a decision. I think you should go to the cops, and then either stay with Tom and me, or get out of town. Don't go to your family. That's the next place Dean would look."

Lydia shook more. Her body felt cold from head to toe despite the heat. She looked down, not finding any words.

"She's right," Bri said. "We love you, and we want you safe. I'm really scared for you."

Still shaking, Lydia stared at her sandals. "I do have a bag in my trunk."

"Smart girl," Bri said. "I think you know what you need to do."

"If you don't want to go to the cops, give me all the details you have, and I'll call in an anonymous tip. They have to start looking into this— before anyone else gets hurt. The last thing I want is to see something happen to one of my friends."

"Then what? What if they find him guilty?" Tears blurred Lydia's vision.

Savannah squeezed her hand hard. "Then the world is a safer place."

"And you can go back home," said Bri.

"I don't know if I can." Lydia felt sick.

"Where else would you go?" asked Savannah.

Lydia shrugged. "I doubt I could afford the house without Dean's money."

"Then sell it, and buy a cute condo." Bri gave Lydia a forced smile. "You could have fun with that."

"Right." Lydia flatly.

"Oh, I know. You could hang out with that horse guy," Bri said. "Remember from the HOA meeting? Some girl's brother? His name was Tony or something."

"Toby," Lydia corrected. "He's too young for me. Plus I wouldn't want to drag him into my messed up life."

"Don't worry about what you're going to do later," Savannah said. "You need to decide where you're going to sleep tonight, and whether you're going to call the cops or if I'm going to."

"I'm going to throw up."

"You can do that later." Savannah stood, pulling Lydia with her. "First, tell me what you're going to do."

"I…I'll find a hotel somewhere." Lydia's head spun.

"And…?" asked Savannah.

"There's no way I can call the cops. I just can't. I'm too shaken."

"Okay, then I'll do it."

"But what if they want to question me?" Lydia asked. "Will it look suspicious if I'm not home?"

"Why would they suspect you for anything?" Bri asked. "You weren't with him any of those times?"

Lydia laughed bitterly. "You know as well as I do that I haven't gone anywhere with him."

"Then you're fine," Bri said. "Just take care of yourself, and make yourself available if the police want to ask you anything. No one is going to blame you for trying to get away. If anything, they might question why you stayed after figuring it out."

"Because I didn't want to believe my husband was capable of such things." Lydia glared at her friend. "Anyone could understand that."

"I know, I'm just pointing out something they might ask. You need to be prepared for anything."

"You should get going," Savannah said. "And don't stay anywhere close."

"Do you think he's going to go after them?" Fear and guilt tore at her. "Should I warn them?"

"No," Bri said. "Let Dean see their genuine expressions. He'll know they're not hiding anything."

Lydia hated the idea, but knew that Bri was probably right.

"Call us when you check in somewhere." Savannah kissed Lydia's cheek. "Then I'll call the cops. Or maybe I'll call first? What do you think?"

"I can't think." Lydia continued to shake.

"Everything is going to be okay," Bri said. "Dean will be locked away before we know it, and then you can live your life again. We'll help you find some wonderful single guy. Sound good?"

Lydia took a deep breath. "I guess."

They walked back to Lydia's car in silence.

"Whatever you do, don't go back home," Bri said.

"I know."

"Get at least an hour away," Savannah said.

"Okay."

"I'm serious." Savannah looked into her eyes.

Lydia nodded. "I promise."

Savannah and Bri hugged her, and then Lydia got into her car and drove out of the parking lot.

Fear

BRI WATCHED AS Lydia's car disappeared from sight, and then stared at Savannah. "What are we going to do?"

She shook her head. "I'm scared out of my mind. Do you think we should've told her about Cara?"

"No. That poor girl has more than enough on her plate. She'll find out about Cara and Dean eventually, but she needs to deal with this first."

"That's true. I couldn't imagine throwing in the betrayal of a best friend on top of everything else."

"What are we going to do about Cara?" Bri asked. "She's probably with Dean."

"And she's probably at more risk than Lydia."

"It depends on how badly Dean wants the baby," Bri said. "He was pretty upset about not being able to have a baby with Lydia, right? If he really wants a child, Cara could be okay."

Savannah shook her head. "I knew Dean was a jerk. I mean, who is so obvious about having affairs? But I never would have guessed this in a million years."

"Me, neither," Bri said. "And now two of our friends are in danger. What are you going to tell the police?"

"I don't really have anything yet. I should've had Lydia write everything down for me before she left. I'm just not thinking straight."

"None of us is. I really think we should warn Cara."

"She won't even take our calls," Savannah said.

"I'll leave her a message telling her it's life and death."

"And risk having her tell Dean?" asked Savannah.

"We have to do something." Bri's stomach twisted in knots. "I think

I'm going to be sick. Do you really think Dean is capable of murder?"

Savannah looked at Bri. "I think anyone is capable of anything given the right circumstances. Some people just have a taste for blood. He might have accidentally killed the first one, and then decided he liked it."

"But why keep Lydia around?" asked Bri. "He's never hidden his disdain for her since their fertility problems."

"She probably makes a good alibi." Savannah shrugged. "Nobody's suspected anything up until now, right? We wouldn't know anything unless Lyds found those papers."

"We need to warn Cara."

"What if she doesn't believe us?" Savannah asked.

"Then it's out of our hands," Bri said, "but I couldn't live with myself if I didn't try to warn her."

"What if he goes after us?" Savannah asked. "Lydia seems to think that he might. If we tell Cara, and she doesn't believe us…."

"Then she tells Dean," Bri finished. "I don't think he would be after us so much as Lydia."

"She's hiding. If he can't find her, he could go after us."

Blood drained from Bri's face. "I can't put my family at risk. My girls."

"No. Don't. I'll take care of all this. I'll even tell Cara that you don't know anything."

"She won't believe you. Lydia tells me everything."

They stared at each other, not saying anything. Bri's mind raced. Part of her wished Lydia hadn't said anything because now she had to worry about her kids' safety. Would Dean go after them to keep himself from being caught? On the other hand, Bri was glad Lydia told them. Otherwise, Lydia might have gone back home to Dean. How could she have stayed with him for even a minute after discovering the clippings? And how could she have kept it from them for so long?

"What should we do?" Savannah asked.

Bri shook her head. "I'm scared."

"Me, too. I can't believe we have a killer in the neighborhood."

"At least he hasn't gone after anyone there. Everyone's accounted for."

"I need to talk with Tom," Savannah said. "He'll know what to do."

"And I should tell Corey. Maybe between the four of us, we can figure something out."

"Bri, I think you should just go home and pretend like everything's normal. Keep your family out of it. I'll talk with Tom and some of our biker friends. You'd be surprised at how resourceful some of them are."

Bri thought of her sweet girls. "Thank you, Savannah."

Agitated

CARA PACED THE living room. Where was Dean? He had promised to be back over an hour ago, and her calls kept going straight to voice mail. Had she done something to piss him off?

She rubbed her stomach, trying to calm down. Her blood pressure was going up, and she knew she had to keep it under control.

How could Dean put this kind of stress on her? He had promised to take care of her and the baby. He'd been spending so much time with Lydia when he was in town. It just didn't make any sense. They couldn't stand each other, until suddenly they showed up at that HOA meeting holding hands.

What if she had changed her mind and was trying to save their marriage? Why would she do that all of a sudden? Because she finally figured out that the guy she'd fallen in love with had moved on for good?

Or what if she knew about the baby? Lydia was too smart for her own good. It was only a matter of time before she put two and two together, and she might have already done so.

Cara pulled out her phone. If she wasn't so upset, she'd call Savannah or Bri. They'd certainly called enough times. Maybe they already knew that Ethan had kicked her out. They weren't ones to leave anything alone, so it was only a matter of time before they went to her house.

Ethan was working from home this week, so he would have answered, and probably told them that Cara wasn't his problem anymore.

She found Dean's number and called it. Straight to voice mail again. What was he doing that was so important? He had to have known she needed to talk to him. He would probably be pissed at how many times she'd called, but Cara didn't care. She just needed to know what was going on.

She was half-tempted to call her friends back and have some girl time, but she would be worried about Dean the entire time. Cara called him a couple more times, and then texted him to call her.

This wasn't going to get her anywhere. Pacing and calling only added to her stress. If she wasn't pregnant, she would grab a glass of wine, or maybe the whole bottle, to calm her nerves. Since that wasn't an option, she needed to figure out another way to relax until Dean finally decided to get back to her.

Cara grabbed the remote and flipped through the channels, looking for a movie or something to distract her. Nothing looked interesting. They hadn't signed up for Netflix yet, so she was stuck with cable. She went upstairs to find her tablet. She still had her account with Ethan on there.

She turned on the tablet and then clicked the app. It prompted her to sign in. When she did, it said she had the wrong password. Ethan had already shut her out of that. Cara threw it on the bed.

What now? She went back downstairs, tempted to call Dean again, but she knew he wouldn't answer. She sat down and flipped through the channels again. After going through all the channels at least twice, she finally settled on a reality show about a woman with three husbands. Wasn't one enough? Cara couldn't imagine life with more than one, and after watching the show, she was even more convinced she couldn't do it.

It must have been a marathon because one show after another played. After the first one, Cara got into it, and almost forgot about Dean. Almost. Every time she heard something outside, she jumped to the window. After a while, she stopped checking.

Eventually, it started getting dark outside, and Cara got hungry. She went to the kitchen and realized how little food they actually had. She needed to go shopping. She made a sandwich and settled in for another episode, glad to know someone else had more drama in her life than Cara.

Just after she finished the sandwich, she heard something outside. Cara didn't bother checking, knowing that it wasn't Dean. Then she heard the lock in the front door.

Relief swept through her. Finally, he was home.

The door slammed. "Can't you take a hint?"

Cara's heart sank. "What do you mean?"

He came into the room, his eyes narrowed. "When I don't answer the phone. It means I can't talk. That's not an invitation to keep calling—over and over again."

"But I—"

"One message or text is sufficient. Do you understand?"

"Dean, I—"

His brows furrowed. "Do you understand?"

"Yes."

"I'm a busy man. A lot of people need a lot from me. From work and my personal life. I don't need my phone going off every two minutes."

"I get it. I was just worried."

"Were you afraid I was with Lydia?"

The look in his eyes scared her. "I just didn't know where you were."

"And if I was available to tell you, I would have."

She nodded. "I understand."

"Do you?"

"Yes. I won't do it again."

"Good."

He stared at the TV. "What are you watching?"

"Just a stupid show. I needed something to distract myself with."

Dean picked up the remote and turned it off.

"What's going on?" she asked.

He continued to pace. "I think she knows. It's the only explanation."

"What?"

"Everything. She knows everything."

"Who?" Cara's pulse raced.

"Lydia."

"What? About us?"

"No." Anger covered his face, and he paced back and forth, furrowing his eyebrows.

Cara backed up, watching him. She didn't dare ask what Lydia knew about—not when Dean was acting like this. She took a few deep breaths to calm herself. Once she was sure she could speak steadily, she went over to him and put her hand on his shoulder. "Want to talk about it?" she asked in her most soothing tone. "Let me help you."

He turned and glared at her. "You can't."

She moved closer to him, rubbing his arm. "I can try. Let me in, Dean. What's going on?"

Turning, he slapped her. Cara backed up, holding the spot on her face. It heated up by the second. "What did you do that for?"

He smacked her again, this time on the other cheek.

"Dean!"

He grabbed her shoulders and shook her. "You need to stop, Cara."

"No, you do."

Dean shoved her against the wall. "You don't understand the pressure I'm under. If Lydia...." He turned around and punched the wall, putting his fist through it. "I thought I had her where I wanted her. Everything was fine, but I don't think it is. I'm going to crumble under this pressure. I had everything under control."

Cara moved away from him.

"I've held it together so well until now," he muttered. "If she rats me out, that's it. Everything is over."

"Wh...what can I do?" Cara asked, shaking.

"There's nothing you can do. Nothing. Just shut up and give me space. That's all I need."

"Fine. You have it." She walked toward the stairs, still grasping her face. Cara moved slowly, giving him the opportunity to apologize or explain himself, but he did neither.

She stopped at the bottom of the stairs and watched him pace. Tears stung Cara's eyes. What had happened to make him hit her? He would have to explain at some point. She wasn't going to raise her child around someone like that. If he ever laid a hand on her again, he would regret it.

Cara wouldn't hesitate to call the cops and have domestic violence put on his record. That would show him.

She stepped onto the first stair, still watching. He paced, muttering to himself and looking out the window. She couldn't make out most of what he said. She caught more of "she knows," but not much else.

What could Lydia know? Maybe Cara shouldn't have ignored all of

Bri's and Savannah's phone calls. If Dean wouldn't tell her what he was so upset about, then Cara would return their calls—assuming Dean calmed down. Watching him, he appeared to be growing angrier by the minute.

Cara took a deep breath and then walked back over to the couch. "Would you like me to make something to eat?"

He turned, stopped, and stared at her. "Do I look like I want to sit down and eat?" He practically shouted, making Cara jump. "Could women be any more stupid?"

Cara bit her tongue, her face still stinging. She needed to keep a calm head. "Well, if you decide that you want some company, let me know." She spun around, and went up the stairs, and into the bedroom, closing the door behind her. She wanted to slam it—show him how angry she was at his behavior—but she didn't want to risk angering him further. Whatever Lydia had done, he couldn't get past it. The last thing she needed was to add to it, or to her stinging face.

She walked to the window, hoping the scenery could calm her down. Instead, she was distracted by neighbors chatting and laughing. Probably the same ones who had given her such a warm welcome before.

Cara turned around and paced. Now they were both pacing. Why wouldn't Dean just tell her what bothered him? He said she was such a good listener, that he'd never felt so understood by anyone before. Or maybe he'd just wanted something else. Who knew? How well did she really know him?

The front door slammed, and Cara went back to the window. Dean walked toward his car, ignoring the overly-friendly neighbors who were obviously flirting with him.

Was he leaving? Cara pressed her face against the glass, trying to see what he was up to in the car. Maybe he was only getting something to bring back into the house.

He leaned against his car and lit a cigarette. When had he started smoking? At least he was outside, keeping the fumes away from her baby. She watched with pleasure as he ignored the neighbors flirting.

Cara took some deep breaths. She needed to think of something to say so she could calm him down when he came back inside. Whatever Lydia had done, Cara would have to undo. Typical selfish Lydia. Cara wouldn't miss her. The other girls—yeah, she was going to miss Savannah and Bri.

She could already see the judging looks on their faces because Cara was having Dean's baby. Once they found out they had a house now, they would probably band together against her.

Cara needed to find new friends, but it wouldn't be from the new neighborhood. Those were the type of women she wanted nothing to do with.

Dean threw the cigarette to the ground and stepped on it. Cara prepared herself for what she would say. She needed to convince him that she was safe to talk to. She wouldn't give him grief for whatever was going on with Lydia.

Instead of going back to the house, Dean turned around, got into the car, and drove off.

Cara stared in disbelief as his car disappeared from sight.

Missing

"YOU GIRLS STAY right here," Bri said, looking around the rec room. There was no reason for her to worry about anyone getting in there. They were on the top level, there was only a small window going outside, and no way to get to it from the backyard.

"Okay, Mom."

"Sure."

They both smiled at her, and then turned to the movie Bri had put on. Her heart pounded in her chest. She still hadn't heard back from Lydia, and Cara continued to avoid her calls.

There was no way Dean would know Bri had told Lydia to leave. He couldn't know. It just wasn't possible. She walked down to the front door, and double-checked the security system.

Corey came over, and wrapped his arms around her from behind. "It's going to be okay, honey."

Bri turned and looked at his beautiful face. "Not even you can help me relax right now, babe." She ran her palm against his soft, chocolaty skin. "Not this time."

He frowned, but then gave her a kiss. "I'll do whatever I can."

"Just keep the girls safe."

"Bri, if Dean is dumb enough to come to our house, he won't live to tell about it. He won't even make it inside."

She checked her phone again. "I hate not knowing where either one of them is. Now that I know what he's capable of...."

"Lydia's probably safe. If she's smart, she ditched her phone. He could easily track her, you know."

Bri's heart jumped into her throat. "I never even thought of that. And what about her car? It has all kinds of wireless capabilities. Could he track that, too?"

Corey squeezed her. "If he really wanted to."

"What are we going to do?" Bri asked. Her stomach twisted into tight knots.

"Stay right here, and keep our family safe."

"I don't know how long I can do that, Cor."

"You have no choice." He pulled her closer into his embrace. "I'm not letting you out of my sight."

"If I don't hear from Lyds, I'm going after her."

Corey kissed her ear. "You don't know where she is."

Bri pulled away. "But I can find her. I know she didn't go near her family. She probably went in the opposite direction. If Dean goes looking, he's probably going straight to her family."

"Wait for her to call. She's smart enough to pick up a disposable phone. Give her time."

"I'm going to throw up."

"Let me make you some tea. Chamomile?"

Bri shook her head. "And women say there is no perfect man."

Corey grinned. "I try."

The doorbell rang.

Bri and Corey exchanged a worried look. Bri's stomach twisted tighter, and she was sure she'd lose control of her bladder.

"Let me." Corey walked past her, and looked into the peephole. "It's Chad Mercer. He's safe, right?"

"Chad?" Bri asked. Things had to have gone from bad to worse if Chad was at their door. "Let him in."

Corey opened the door and exchanged greetings with their neighbor. Chad came in, and Corey closed the door behind them.

Bri looked Chad over, trying to gauge the seriousness of the situation. "What's going on, Chad?"

"Can we sit?"

Corey pointed toward their front room.

"I'll be right there," Bri said. She needed to empty her bladder before talking with Chad. Her mind raced with the worst possible scenarios. It had to be bad news if Chad was there. There was no other explanation.

When Bri got to the front room, Corey and Chad were discussing the latest Mariner's game.

"What's going on, Chad?" Bri asked, desperately trying to keep her voice steady. She sat next to Corey, who took her hand.

Chad cleared his throat, and then looked at Bri. "I'm sure you know that Lydia and I developed a friendship some time ago."

"If you want to call it that," Corey said.

Bri nudged him. "Yes. What's going on?"

"I'm really worried about her. Is she okay?" Chad looked pale.

"Why are you worried? Did she contact you?" Bri asked.

Chad raked his hands through his hair, and then took a deep breath. "She came to me at the party earlier."

Bri nodded. "That's right. I saw the announcement in the HOA bulletin. Sorry we couldn't make it."

"No problem. But Lydia stopped by, and she wasn't herself. Not at all. She said something that made me think she was scared of Dean, and she was basically saying goodbye." He pulled some of his hair into his fists. "It wasn't like…." Chad took a deep breath, still grasping his hair. "It was like she didn't expect to see me again, ever."

Corey gave her a worried look.

"Is she in danger?" Chad asked.

"What exactly did she tell you?" Bri asked.

"Not very much, and I was distracted hosting a party. It wasn't until the party was over that the severity of her reaction hit me."

Corey wrapped his arm around Bri, and looked at Chad. "When she said goodbye, did you think she was moving away or in danger? Did you get the feeling she thought she might never return alive?"

Chad finally let go of his hair, and shook his head. "I don't know. But she said something about Dean having a secret, and she had to get away. She was definitely scared… and saying a final goodbye. Do you know why she's scared of him?"

Bri nodded. "I'm the one who told her to leave town."

"Did he find out about us?" Chad asked, looking like he was going to be sick.

"No," Bri said. "You don't have to worry about Alyssa finding out. No one's going to say anything."

"Would he hurt Lydia?" Chad asked.

"He's never laid a finger on her," Bri said, "but that could definitely change."

They all sat in silence.

Finally, Chad looked back at them. "Where did she go?"

"We don't know," Bri said. "It's safer that way. Dean can't force it out of anyone."

"What do you mean?" asked Chad.

"Lydia discovered that he's not above hurting people," Bri said. "That's all I'm going to say. It's not my place."

"We have to do something."

"What?" Corey asked.

"Something." Chad looked around. "We can't just sit around doing nothing."

"Not much else to do," Corey said. "We have to wait until she contacts us."

Chad swore. "That's not good enough."

"Go back to your family. If there's anything we think you can help with, we'll let you know."

"Look," Chad said, staring at Corey. "I'm not proud of what I did, okay? My marriage wasn't in a good place at the time, and I made a bad decision. But none of that changes the fact that I care about Lydia. I can't just go back home and pretend like northing's wrong. I just can't. I need to do something."

"That's what we have to do," Bri snapped. "Just sit and wait. Keep our kids safe, and hope the best for Lydia. No one knows where she went, so we can't even go after her."

Chad sat up taller. "You think your kids are in danger?"

"Anyone who has helped Lydia could be in harm's way."

"Even my kids?" Chad asked.

"Only if Dean thinks you've aided her."

Chad swore again. "I've got a whole group of teenagers in my house right now."

Corey looked directly at him. "Then I suggest you get back home and set your alarm."

"Let me give you my number, in case you need anything." Chad stood up.

"It's in the HOA directory, right?" Bri asked.

"Yeah."

"We'll call you if anything comes up. I promise." Bri stood. "We'll see you to the door."

"She's going to be all right, isn't she?"

"We can only hope," Corey said.

They walked Chad to the door. Once he was outside, he said, "Call me if you need anything."

"We will," Corey said, and then closed and locked the door. He turned to Bri. "Can you believe him?"

"He's worried about her."

"He doesn't have the right to be."

"I think he can't help it. It's sweet that he still cares about her."

"Sweet?" Corey asked. "He cheated on his wife with her and then decided to go back to being a family man."

"He also gave her happiness in a time when she had none. We all know how much Dean cheated on Lydia."

Corey shook his head. "I have no pity for any man who cheats on his wife. None."

Bri wrapped her arms around him. "And I love that about you. But at the same time, I think Lydia's situation was different. I mean, really. She married a serial killer."

"Doesn't excuse Chad's behavior."

Bri pulled out her phone. "Let's worry about Lydia instead of Chad, okay?"

Corey took a deep breath. "Fine. Have you tried calling Cara or Lydia recently?"

"I've called so many times already. They both know I'm trying to get a hold of them, unless they've gotten rid of their phones."

"Maybe they have. Lydia's on the run, and I wouldn't be surprised if Ethan had Cara's phone turned off. What's going on in this neighborhood?" Corey shook his head. "So much cheating and deception."

"Dean's at the bottom of all of this."

"I always knew there was something off about him."

"When?" Bri asked. "Like what?"

"Just a feeling."

Reality

LYDIA PEEKED OUT the curtain, checking on her car. She hated parking out in the open but had no other choice. All of her credit cards and bank accounts had been frozen. She had to stay at the cheapest motel she could find, and she barely had enough cash for one night.

It was too early to worry about what she would do tomorrow, but she would need to figure something out. She would likely have to sleep in her car or go to her brother. Without money, she had no other options. Not unless she wanted to go back to Dean, but after disappearing—and having her accounts messed with—she couldn't do that.

He had to have known something was wrong. Why else would he do that to her? He wouldn't keep her from their money unless he had good reason.

She needed to cut her losses.

What she needed was to find an actual piece of evidence to put Dean at any one of the murders. Just being in town wasn't proof of anything. Not even being in town when all of them happened meant anything. For all Lydia knew, it just meant that she had an overactive imagination.

She could just picture a room full of cops laughing at her, calling her a bored and neglected housewife. Someone might even suggest she write screenplays for a living.

No. She needed something solid. She had grabbed a manila folder of receipts from Dean's office and put it in her trunk, meaning to go through them when she was in Oregon. If he had been stupid enough to save one from the workplace of any of those girls, that should be enough.

Just one clue to say this was serious. Something they couldn't ignore. Then she could leave it to the professionals to find other clues. She walked around the little motel room, feeling like a caged animal.

Why was it that she was stuck in there, hiding, while Dean roamed free? She looked out the window again, wanting to go out to the car and grab the folder of receipts. She couldn't risk it. If she was going to leave the room, she needed to wait until dark.

Lydia pulled her new laptop out of the bag, and turned it on. There was supposed to be free wi-fi, but the lady at the desk had told her it wasn't that great. The cheap computer came to life, and Lydia watched as it searched for a wireless signal. Finally, it found one, and she connected.

She looked through her fake online persona's emails and social media accounts. Some of the friends and family of the victims had accepted her requests. She didn't see Angie's, but that wasn't a surprise. She hadn't trusted Lydia. That much had been clear.

Lydia relaxed as she read through the emails, and then searched her news feed for anything revealing. There was nothing she could see that lead to Dean, but it wouldn't be that easy.

A scuffling noise outside caught Lydia's attention. She closed the laptop, went over to the door, and looked out the peephole. She couldn't see anything.

She heard another noise.

Lydia looked at the door to make sure all the locks and chains were in place. The mere fact that there were so many of them only made her feel less secure. She was used to hotels with key cards and security cameras. She hadn't seen a camera anywhere, and the key to open her room was so old and rusty, Lydia was sure it was older than her.

She watched from the peephole for a few minutes, and after not hearing or seeing anything, she went back to the stiff bed and reopened the laptop.

It was time to get serious. She got her phone and scrolled through the pictures until she found one of Dean. She didn't have a lot of him, but at least this one was a nice, clear shot of his face. She sent it to her fake email address, and before long, she had sent his photo to as many of the victims' relatives as she could find, asking if they had ever seen him.

Her heart raced. Could doing that be illegal? If not, then it was risky either way. If Dean found out... he wasn't going to. Not before she was able to go to the police. Someone had to have seen him. Even if just one person had a flicker of recognition, that would be something.

He had to have made a mistake somewhere along the line, and Lydia would figure out what that was and use it to bring him to justice. If he went to jail, not only would the world be a safer place, but she would be able to return home. Like Bri had mentioned, she would probably have to sell the house and get a condo, but it would be better than living in a trailer park again.

She couldn't go back to that after having lived in a huge house with a weekly maid service. It just wasn't possible. She'd suck it up in the smelly motel, but that was it. There was no way she would return to her old life. It was so far in the past, it felt like it had been someone else's life, not hers.

A new message. It was regarding the picture of Dean she'd sent out. Lydia clicked on it, her heart racing. Could it be the clue she'd been searching for already? Or another dead end?

The message was from Sam, the cousin of Jessica Aldridge, the last victim that Lydia knew about.

Lydia read the message, unable to make sense of the words. She took several deep breaths. It was time to focus. Her mind spun, making it impossible.

Look at the words. Just pay enough attention to make sense of them.

She stared at the message, focusing on her breaths. Heart pounding, she studied each word one by one. Jessica's cousin recognized Dean. She had been in the library where Jessica worked when Dean approached her, asking to use the internet. She got him set up, and before long, Dean had Jessica laughing.

Lydia read each word again. Sam didn't know if Jessica had gone anywhere with Dean after work because they didn't talk about him when Sam left. They weren't close, and he had just said goodbye on his way out.

He asked Lydia if she thought the man in the picture had anything to do with the murder.

Lydia couldn't get her fingers to move. Now she had actual proof that Dean had had contact with one of the victims. That was probably enough to go to the police. She sat on the bed and shook, so cold that her teeth chattered.

She closed the laptop, and then grabbed her travel bag. Lydia pulled some clothes out and brought them to her face. Tears pouring, she screamed as loud as she could into them. She screamed again, and then again.

How could this be? How could she have married a serial killer? Why had she been so blind as to miss the signs? She should have questioned him being away from home so much.

Lydia had fought him at first, saying that no one should travel so often—that three days a month at home wasn't right. But he kept getting irritated, saying that she was overreacting and being a typical emotional woman.

Not wanting to hear that anymore, she stopped asking about it. And eventually, people stopped asking her about him being gone all the time. It was just their normal, and once she met Chad, Lydia had no complaints about Dean's schedule again.

Now she knew how stupid she had been, ignoring the feeling that something was wrong.

She screamed into the clothes again. If she had been more diligent, some of those women could still be alive. She screamed again.

Lydia couldn't do anything about the past, but she could prevent anyone else from being killed at her husband's hand. She opened the laptop and took a screen shot of the email and sent it to her phone. She couldn't risk only having the email in one place. Plus, she had the pictures of the clippings on her phone.

The only decision she had left was whether to go to the cops in this town, or the ones closer to where they lived. It would probably make more sense to go back home and talk to the ones there. On the other hand, she was already here. If need be, the local cops could take what she had and share with the ones back home.

Her stomach turned at the thought of going back and being near Dean. She didn't ever want to see him again—there was no way she could even look at him. Not now. He may have been able to sweet-talk her before, when she had a reasonable doubt. That was gone now.

She looked everything over on the laptop before shutting it down, and then she packed the clothes back into the bag. She needed to get to the police as soon as possible. The longer she was gone, the more time it gave Dean to figure out that she knew. He could flee town or worse, go after her.

Shaking, she grabbed everything and headed out the door. Just as she closed it behind her, someone said her name.

Scared

BRI SAT WITH her family, watching a movie she couldn't focus on. Every few minutes, she got up and looked out a front window. Then the sides and back. Everything looked normal each time, but her nerves felt afire.

What if Dean figured out that they knew about the killings? He would probably stop at nothing to shut them up. Or hurt Lydia. He was a cold-blooded murderer. What did he care about Bri or her family?

She made her way back into the rec room, and caught Corey's attention. She indicated for him to come out into the hall with her. He kissed the top of both girls' heads, and then joined Bri.

"What's going on?"

"I think we should leave."

"And go where, exactly?" he asked.

"I don't care. Anywhere other than here." Bri lowered her voice. "There's a killer in the neighborhood, and we're one of the few people who know his secret."

"He's not going to come after us, and if he tries, I'll stop him."

Bri's vision grew blurry from tears. "Corey, he's a killer. Don't you get that?"

"Has Dean killed a man?"

"Not that I know of. What does that have to do with anything?"

Corey raised an eyebrow. "Men like him are wimps. They go after those who are weaker than them. I'll bet if you look into the victims, they're all people he knew he could overpower. He gets them alone, probably corners them to where they can't escape, and maybe drugs them. Do you think he can take on this?" Corey flexed in several different positions.

Bri cracked a smile, even though she was on edge. "I suppose you have a point."

"Look, honey, if it'll make you feel better, I'll call Tom. They'll drop everything and come over. You think Dean will take on the two of us?"

"You and Tom? Not a chance."

"So, you'd feel better if they were here?" asked Corey.

Bri looked into the rec room. The girls were giggling at the TV. She turned back to Corey. "I would."

Corey pulled her into a hug, and then kissed the top of her head. "Then I'll call them." He pulled his phone from a pocket and called Tom. "Why don't you guys come on over? We'll order pizza. .... Bri's really scared, too. ... Yeah, bring the drinks. .... Cool. See you then."

"They're coming?" Bri asked, relief flooding her.

He kissed her on the lips. "Go in there and sit with the girls. I'm going to order pizza and wait by the door for them."

"What are you going to do if you see Dean?"

"Make him wish he'd never been born. Go on."

Bri went and sat with the girls. Elsie, the youngest, climbed into her lap. Bri wrapped her arms around her, holding her tight. Dean wouldn't dare come in with four adults and two kids. Corey was right—he would never try anything with Corey and Tom there. They were intimidating when they had to be, and they were a lot bigger than Dean. Two Deans probably couldn't fight off one of them.

"You okay, Mommy?" Elsie asked.

"Yeah, sweetie." Bri kissed the top of her head. She tried to get into the movie. It was a kids' comedy about a talking otter trying to escape the zoo using a broken furnace. They'd seen it at least a hundred times.

After a few scenes played out, Bri heard the door open downstairs. She relaxed further when Tom's and Savannah's voices drifted upstairs. They were laughing with Corey about something.

Bri sat Elsie on a bean bag, and then kissed both girls before heading downstairs.

Savannah and Tom both gave her a hug, and then they all headed into the kitchen. Bri pulled Savannah aside as the men got the table ready for the pizza.

"Have you heard from Cara or Lydia?" Bri asked.

"I wish."

"Something's wrong," Bri said. "I can just feel it. I don't know which one is in more danger."

"Probably Cara, since Lydia's out of town. Wherever Cara's staying, it's probably with Dean somewhere. Lydia's always thought he had a place somewhere else, right?"

Bri nodded, frowning. "I wish Cara would at least text us and say she's okay. Does she think we're just trying to annoy her?"

"She probably has no clue that Dean's killing people," Savannah said. "For all we know, she thinks we're siding with Lydia and just want to chew her out."

"Cara can be so selfish sometimes." Bri gritted her teeth. "I just want to punch her."

"Yeah. Me, too."

Bri's phone rang. She and Savannah exchanged a look.

"Who is it?" Savannah asked.

"Unknown number," Bri said. She ran to the front room and accepted the call. "Hello?"

"Bri?" asked a familiar male voice.

"Who is this?" Bri asked. It didn't sound like Dean.

"Sorry. It's Chad."

Bri wanted to roll her eyes.

"Who is it?" mouthed Savannah, coming into the room.

"Chad," Bri mouthed back. Then she spoke into the phone. "What do you want?"

"Have you guys heard back from her?" asked Chad.

"No. Why are you calling?"

"I'm worried. I have a really bad feeling."

"Just keep your family safe."

"I am," Chad said, "but I keep imagining her getting hurt. We should go to the police. They'll listen to me. I'm on a first-name basis with half the officers there."

"I'm sure you are. Let us handle it, okay?"

"Shouldn't we warn the neighborhood that we have a killer in our midst? People should know."

Bri sighed. "You're wearing me out."

"We don't know where Lydia is, and she knows about his hobby," Chad said. "She's in danger."

"I know that."

"Look, Bri, if you don't go to the police, I will."

"Are you really going to put your marriage on the line? Your wife is going to ask questions."

"I'm a concerned neighbor."

"Right." Bri snorted.

"This is ridiculous." The call ended.

Bri swore.

"What?" Savannah asked.

"I think Chad's going to the cops."

"Maybe that isn't a bad thing."

"I don't know what to think." Bri sat down on a recliner.

Savannah sat on the one next to her. "Well, it's better than this. Waiting…wondering."

Bri looked out the window. "I wish one of them would answer their phones."

"So do I. But they won't, so I think we should just try to enjoy ourselves."

"While our friends are in danger?" Bri asked.

"Well, we do need to keep up a good atmosphere for the girls, right? You don't want them picking up on the fact that something could be wrong." Savannah looked up at the stairs.

Bri followed her gaze, and saw Elsie and Addison standing at the top.

"The movie's over," Addison said.

"Put on a TV show," Bri said. "We'll get you when the pizza's here."

"Pizza!" both girls squealed, and ran off.

"I think they'll provide a good distraction for us." Savannah grinned, but Bri could tell it was forced.

"That they will." Bri looked at her phone again, knowing there were no missed calls.

"Maybe we should stick our phones in a corner, and forget about them for a while," Savannah said.

"What if Lydia or Cara tries to call?"

"There isn't much we'd be able to do for them even if they did, which they won't."

"We might." Bri frowned, staring at the screen.

"Maybe you should look at it harder," Savannah said. "You could will them to call back."

Bri grabbed a throw pillow and chucked it at Savannah's head.

Savannah laughed. "That's more like it. There's the Bri we all know and love."

Bri's phone rang. She looked over at Savannah, and they both exchanged a fearful expression.

Taken

LYDIA FROZE, BUT tried to act natural. "Dean. What are you doing here?"

"What am I doing here? You're the one staying in a fleabag motel. Isn't a place like this beneath you?"

Keeping her eyes on him, she focused on the periphery. She would have to run, but he would likely catch up given the sandals she had on.

"Why are you here?" she asked. "I didn't think you were back in town already."

"A little birdie told me you were staying here. I didn't believe him, but it looks like I was proven wrong."

Still taking in the surroundings, Lydia asked, "But why are you looking for me?"

"What are *you* doing here?" he snarled.

"Research." She continued to look for the best way of escape.

"For what?" Dean sneered.

She stared into his eyes. "My job."

"You mean that column you write...Layla?"

Her eyes widened. Dean knew about that? Even her pen name?

Dean laughed. "I know a lot more about you than you think."

Lydia flipped her hair behind her shoulder. "Well, I need to get going so I can turn in my article in time."

"How are they going to pay you with all your accounts on hold?"

She narrowed her eyes. "You did that?"

"You left me with no other choice."

Her mind spun. "Wait. How did you find me here? Did you follow me?"

"All I had to do was call the cell phone provider and tell them we lost the phone." He shrugged. "You're not the only resourceful one."

"I learned from the best." Lydia stepped back.

Dean stepped closer. "But you haven't seen all my tricks."

Lydia swallowed. "I have a good imagination."

"I know you do. Like with that *coupon* you found?"

"Oh, that?" Lydia asked. "I thought you were getting back into golf. No?"

"When was the last time I was into golf, Lyds?" He leaned in closer, and she smelled perfume on him.

"Not since before you started traveling, and whatever else you've been doing."

Dean laughed, and Lydia took advantage of his moment of distraction. She turned around and ran. He didn't miss a beat—she heard his footsteps not a moment later. She dropped her bags and darted down some stairs.

She could hear him close behind. Between her sandals and the stairs, she knew he had the advantage since he was in sneakers.

"What are you running from?" Dean called. "Think you have a reason to be scared of me?" He fingers brushed against the back of her bare arm.

Lydia ignored him, put her hand over the railing and started skipping steps. She might fall, but it was worth the risk if she could get enough ahead of him.

She looked toward her parked car. That was out of the question because she'd dropped everything. She made it to the last step without losing her balance.

"Why not give up now?" Dean asked. "You know I'm going to catch you eventually."

Lydia kicked her sandals off, running faster. The hot pavement stung, but it was better than being slowed down by the footwear.

"Hey!"

She looked back to see Dean stumbling over a sandal. Good. He corrected his footing, and Lydia turned her attention to what was in front of her. She was nearing a wall, so she would either have to go right and stay on the sidewalk, or dart underneath some stairs. She couldn't risk being cornered, so she followed the sidewalk.

The pavement tore the skin on Lydia's feet, but she ignored the pain. Dean yelled at her to stop, but she kept going. Did he really expect her to surrender that easily?

She reached the sidewalk by the main road. With any luck, she would run into another pedestrian and get help. Cars would be of no use. They zoomed by at about fifty miles an hour. The only hope they offered her was that someone might see her running from Dean, and later recognize them if Lydia ended up missing.

They ran past a strip mall, and then there was a break of trees. It looked like it led to some woods behind the mall and possibly the motel, too. Lydia regretted kicking off the sandals as she ran over the rocky dirt. Some rocks were sharp and cut into her skin.

At least she was able to leave behind DNA evidence if anyone ever went looking. She tried to go faster, but couldn't because of the painful rocks. Dean was getting closer—she could hear his breathing from behind.

"Lydia, stop. We need to talk."

"Talk? You just want to talk?" She squeezed between some close trees, hoping he would have a harder time getting through than her.

She looked back, and saw that he managed without much difficulty. It was only a matter of time before he caught her. Lydia knew she had to come to terms with it, and decide what she would do to fight him off or try to get attention from anyone who might be close enough to hear them.

Lydia climbed over a mossy log, and the soft carpeting felt good on her pained feet. She wished she could stop, but Dean continued to get closer.

"Let's talk about this, Lydia. I don't want to hurt you."

"Really? Is that why you're chasing me through woods? Why I had to drop all my stuff?"

"I didn't tell you to run."

She shook her head, and continued going. She felt his fingers brush against the back of her shoulder. Lydia tried to go faster, but stepped really hard on a sharp rock, and tumbled down to the ground.

Dean reached for her, and she screamed as loud as she could. Her throat was going to hurt in the morning—if she made it that long.

"Stop. Shut up, Lydia. Just let me help you up."

"Why? So you can do to me what you did to the others?"

He grabbed her wrist, and yanked her up. "So, you know about them? How many?"

"Enough." She spit in his face. "How could you?"

Dean wiped his face. "I didn't mean to, not the first time, anyway."

"What? You got a taste for it?"

"Something like that. It started out as just another one-night stand." He laughed. "You'd be surprised how many women are more than happy to do what you weren't."

"What does that have to do with killing them?"

His eyes lit up. "I don't kill most of them. Like I said, the first one was an accident. She started arguing with me and I shoved her. We were at the top of the stairs. I probably don't have to fill in the details. It was a rush to realize how much power I had—I have. I couldn't stop thinking about it, and eventually, I couldn't wait to do it again. So, I did."

"You make me sick. Don't you know the normal response to accidentally killing someone is guilt? Remorse?"

He squeezed her arm. "I was afraid, but then I realized what a rush it is. Life was so stressful back home, but that…that was a thrill."

"So, now you're trying to blame me?"

"Blame? No. If you hadn't turned into the ice queen, I never would have discovered what I was really meant for."

"Are you for real?" Lydia asked.

"Come on. I'll tell you about it in the car."

She pulled away. "I'm not going anywhere with you."

"You have to, Lyds. Now that you know my secret, it's your only choice."

"Why don't you just stop? You have to know it's wrong. That's why you hide it."

He grabbed her arm again, this time squeezing so tight it cut off the circulation.

"That's where you're wrong. I keep it secret because no one understands. They've made something so beautiful illegal."

"Beautiful? You're so full of—"

"You'd have to experience it to understand. That's the problem. Not enough people have gotten the joy."

Lydia shook her head, at a loss for words.

"Let's go back home. You can think about whether you want to join me or if you're going to force me to add you to my list."

There was no chance she would ever join him, but if she pretended to consider, she would be able to buy herself some time. "You want me by your side?"

"Of course I do. Despite our problems, I've never stopped loving you." Still squeezing her arm, he ran his fingers over her cheeks.

Lydia flinched at his touch.

"Let's go." He pulled on her arm, leading her out of the woods.

She didn't say anything, her mind rushing with ways to escape. He would have to let go of her at some point. Then she could run again. Her feet stung and ached, so it would be hard to get away. Maybe there would be others in the parking lot at the motel. She could make enough noise to worry Dean, and he would be forced to let her go.

They came back to the sidewalk, and Lydia looked around. Again, there was no one in sight. Nobody to help her. Once back at the hotel parking lot, he unlocked his car with the remote.

"What about my car?" she asked.

"You were going to leave it here overnight, anyway. I'm sure it'll be fine."

"My stuff. I left it up by the room."

"Ah, that's right. I'll be sure to grab it before we leave."

"My car. Just let me drive it home, Dean. I promise to follow you home."

"You ran away from me, darling. I can't trust you. We'll report it stolen, and have it towed back."

"But, I—"

"Enough. I need to give you some time to think." He clicked his remote again, and the trunk popped open.

Lydia's heart sank, and she turned to look Dean in the eyes. "No, Dean. Don't. Please."

His grip around her arm tightened, and he forced her to walk toward the open trunk. She saw rope and duct tape inside.

Stuck

CARA CALLED DEAN again. She'd lost count of how many calls she'd made already. He would be pissed, but she didn't care. He owed her an explanation. She carried his baby, and he said she was the most special woman in his life. He promised to drop Lydia, but he kept putting that off.

Voice mail.

"Ugh!" Cara paced the bedroom, thinking of their last encounter, and how wonderful it'd been. He truly adored her, even her growing belly. He was a real man—something her husband never would be.

Cara's phone rang. Bri again. When would she and Savannah get the clue? She didn't want to talk to them. Not now.

She still wanted to slap Lydia for that. It made Cara wonder if Lydia knew about them, and it was only a show. Could she be trying to win back her husband because suddenly he seemed valuable again now that Cara wanted him?

Cara laughed. Oh, the irony. All Lydia had was a marriage certificate and a house. Cara rubbed her belly. She had what really mattered— family. She and Dean would forever be connected no matter what. Lydia couldn't give that to him.

A smirk spread across her face thinking about Lydia's face when she found out about Dean being the father of Cara's baby. At first, Cara had felt bad about the whole thing. But that was before Ethan kicked her out of her own house. If he would have let them have their little family, everything would have been fine with Lydia...but now it was different. Cara needed Dean, and that meant war.

It didn't need to be that way. If Lydia had continued hating him, she might have been happy for Cara. She would have been glad to wash her hands of him. Had they been friends still, Cara would have insisted Dean take care of Lydia financially. Not now. She could live on the street for all Cara cared.

Trying to get Dean back after all this time—after he'd fathered her baby.

Cara's phone rang again.

"Will you leave me alone?" she shouted. Cara looked at her phone. Dean.

She almost didn't answer in time. "Dean? What's going on, honey?" she asked as sweetly as possible.

"Why do you keep calling, Cara?"

"You wouldn't answer."

"I left my phone in the car, and come back to more than a dozen missed calls—all from you. Couldn't you see how upset I was before I left the house?"

"Yes," Cara said. "That's why I had to find out if you're okay."

"I'm fine! When I'm busy, just leave me alone. Got it? How much more clear do I need to make myself to you?"

"I was just worried about you."

"Cara, I can take care of myself. I've been doing that for years."

"Okay. When are you coming home?"

"When I get there." His voice was sharp.

"That doesn't tell me anything. Dean, I need you."

"And I need you to be patient. I have things going on that you can't possibly understand."

Cara felt like she'd been slapped. "You'd be surprised how much I understand. I'm not like Lydia."

"Shut up. I don't want you talking about her."

"I can see you're upset." Cara took a deep breath. "When you're ready to come home, I'll be waiting. I might be asleep, but just wake me. Okay?"

"Great. And Cara?"

"Yes?"

"Stop calling me." The call ended.

Cara's blood boiled. How dare he? Did he think she was disposable? When he got back, they needed to have a serious conversation. Talking to her like that was going to end. She wasn't putting up with it for another minute. He could have his cake this time, but then it was over.

Her phone rang again. This time it was Savannah. Cara answered this time. She needed to take her foul mood out on someone.

"What?" Cara demanded.

"Where are you?" Savannah asked. "Bri and I have been trying to reach you all day."

"I've been busy. What's it to you?"

"We're concerned, Cara. Are you okay?"

"Couldn't be better."

"You don't sound good."

"I just had an argument with someone."

"Dean? Is he with you?"

"I don't want to talk about him right now, Savannah."

"We went to your house today. Talked to Ethan."

"So, you know I was kicked out of my own house."

"Honey, we want to help you."

"Don't need it. Dean's taking wonderful care of me."

"Where?"

"We have a house."

"Why am I not surprised?" Savannah asked.

There were muffled noises over the phone. "Cara?" asked Bri. "What's going on? Is Dean with you?"

"Not at the moment. He's due back soon, though."

"You've got to get out of there."

"Why?" Cara demanded. "Because it's hurting Lydia's feelings? She needs to grow up. If she hadn't ignored him all those years, he wouldn't have been so eager to bring me into their bed."

Bri sighed. "Cara, there's a lot about Dean you don't know."

"And there's a lot Lydia doesn't know. Why don't you put her on the phone, and I can tell her."

"We can't. She's not with us—but you're in danger."

"Me?" Cara asked. "Is she going to come after me?"

"No. Dean's dangerous."

"He wouldn't hurt a fly." Cara rubbed the spot where he had slapped her earlier.

"Actually, he would," Bri said. "And he has. He's been killing women for some time."

"What? Shut up, liar."

"Seriously, Cara. We have proof."

"Do you realize the gravity of that accusation?" Cara asked.

"Of course I do. You need to get out of that house before he comes back and decides you're next."

"He loves me."

"Dean only loves himself."

More muffling sounds. "Cara, this is Savannah again. You've got to listen to us. We don't want to see you killed."

"Let's say I was going to listen to you guys, that I believe Dean would hurt me. Where would I go? Back to Ethan?"

"Stay at my house. We have plenty of room."

Cara was quiet. Could they be right? Sure, Dean had a temper. But that didn't make him a killer.

"Think about it, Cara. It explains his traveling. No one is away for work that much. No one."

"You say you have proof?" Cara's hand found its way back to the spot where she'd been slapped.

"Yes, but you have to leave first."

"He's really dangerous?" Cara asked, her voice cracking.

"Worse than that." The fear and worry elevated in Savannah's voice.

"My baby's daddy is a killer?" Cara whispered.

"Yes."

"What have I done?"

"Just get out of there—now. We're at Bri's house."

Cara stood frozen in place. It actually did make sense. His erratic behavior, the long business trips, and the secrecy.

"Cara?" asked Savannah.

"I'm here. I just need to pack a few things."

"Hurry."

Cara ended the call, and then stared at the phone. Was she really about to start her life with a killer? What if her baby got the murderous gene? She stood in place, feeling as though the room moved around her.

At least she hadn't been stupid enough to marry him… yet.

Were the cops after him? Is that why he was out somewhere, not answering his calls? Had he only escaped for a minute to call her back to tell her how stupid he thought she was?

What if he was on his way to the house right then?

She forced her feet into motion. She grabbed a bag, and stuffed some essentials in it. She ran through the house looking for anything she didn't want to leave behind. Most of it was too large to run to the car.

With her arms full, Cara left the house, and ran out front to the car. She threw the bags in and put the key in the ignition, and turned. Nothing happened. Not even the sounds of it trying to start.

Cara tried again a few times before giving up. She pulled the latch to open the hood even though she knew next to nothing about cars. Maybe there would be something obvious. A plug that had come loose or something.

She ran around to the hood, looking over the sight in front of her. Near the middle, a group of wires were sliced in two. Someone had cut the wires. Dean.

Fear and dread tore through her. Cara looked around, expecting to see him ready to pounce. Nobody was in sight.

Tears filling her eyes, she went back into the car and called Bri back.

"Are you on your way?" Bri asked.

"I can't. My car's been tampered with. I can't go anywhere."

"He knew you'd try to leave," Bri said. "Let me send one of the guys to get you."

"Not Tom," Savannah said in the background. "I don't want her near him alone."

Cara's heart sank, but she knew she deserved that.

"You think she's going to try something right now?" Bri asked. Then she spoke into the phone. "What's your address? I'll send Corey."

Home

THE CAR STOPPED, and the engine cut. Lydia stopped squirming. With any luck, Dean would let her out of the trunk. She didn't care where they were. She just needed to find a way to get away from him. Though now, instead of just cut feet, she had rope burns on her ankles and wrists. He'd tied her tight, and then her squirming had only made it worse.

Lydia had hoped to get one of the ropes off so she could break out a tail light or find the emergency release that hopefully hadn't been removed. Knowing Dean, he had probably found a way.

The trunk opened, and Dean appeared standing over her. "Hopefully, the ride home gave you time to think things over."

She stared at him, unable to say anything because of the duct tape over her mouth.

"Are you going to cooperate?"

Lydia mumbled.

"Nod!"

She nodded her head yes.

"Good. I'm glad to hear it." He reached into the trunk, and picked her up, slinging her over his shoulder.

Lydia squirmed.

"Stop that," Dean demanded. "You're going to make me drop you, and that'll hurt worse than your feet. I guarantee it."

She looked down at the hard garage floor and quit fighting. There would be plenty of time for that later. He carried her into the house, and up the stairs, heading for their room. He threw her on the bed.

"I need to know I can trust you."

Lydia nodded again.

"You're not going to try anything funny?"

She shook her head.

"Good. I want nothing more than to have you at my side, Lyds." He pulled the duct tape from her mouth in one quick but painful motion. He threw the tape aside and sat next to her. "Let's talk, and then once I'm sure you're on my side, we'll discuss removing the ropes."

Lydia bit her tongue, not trusting herself to speak.

"Since you know all about my escapades now, I was thinking you could travel with me. Not only could we rebuild our marriage, but you can learn from me how to do this right."

"Killing people?"

He nodded. "There's a method, and it takes practice. I had to learn by making mistakes, but you don't have to."

Lydia squirmed. "Okay. Can you cut these ropes, please? They're really digging into my skin."

"You'll be okay for a little longer, Lyds. It'll build character."

Character? What did he know about that? In a split-second decision, she bit into his arm. She dug in as far as she could, knowing it might be her only chance to hurt him. If nothing else, it would leave a scar so that someday her dental records could prove he'd been the one to hurt her. Maybe it would even lead them to the other women.

Dean let out a cry. "How dare you?" He stood. "I thought you said I could trust you."

"I thought you were going to let me out of these ties."

He swore at her. "So, apparently you're going to take more convincing. You stay here." He shoved her so that she landed on her back.

Dean left the room, closing the door behind him. Lydia heard him slide something in front of it. She looked around the room. There had to be something she could do, or use, to get out of the situation. She rolled around until she could manage to stand.

The window. If she could maneuver her way behind the curtain, maybe she could catch the attention of someone outside. She made her way over to the wall, careful not to hop or make any other noises. She couldn't alert Dean that she was up to something.

She pushed herself against the wall, and then worked her way behind the curtain. The blinds were drawn. She tried to push her head behind them, but that didn't work.

Her heart pounded in her ears. She could hear Dean downstairs. It wouldn't be long before he came back up. She looked around for something—anything. The drawstrings for the blinds hung next to her. Lydia moved over a few steps, and then opened her mouth and bit one of them.

She pulled down with her head, and half of the blind went up, but the other end stayed down. She tried to bite the other string, but let go of the first, causing the blinds so slam down against the window sill.

"Crap!"

Lydia bit the string again and pulled as hard as she could. Again, only half of the blinked went up, but this time it stuck. She pressed her face against the window and looked down. She couldn't see anyone.

"Come on," she muttered. "Someone walk by. Look up."

She heard Dean on the stairs. Lydia moved away from the window. If nothing else, someone might see the blinds messed up, and knock on the door to complain. Some of the HOA members got their panties in a knot over stuff like that. At least she could use that to her advantage. Sandra McMillan would never be able to ignore that, not even if she was late for a meeting. She would have no other choice but to stop and demand the blind was fixed. She might even insist on going upstairs to fix it herself.

Lydia heard the scraping of Dean moving the object away from the doorway. She made her way back to the bed, but didn't have time to sit before Dean opened the door.

"I see you found a way to get off the bed. That's unfortunate because you're going right back there." He held up a knife. It was a gift from their wedding. "I didn't want to have to bring this up here, but you left me no other choice."

Lydia's heart sank. She threw herself onto the bed.

"Good girl," Dean said, his voice smooth. He flipped her over. "See this knife?"

She stared.

He grabbed her hair and yanked. "See it?"

"Yes."

"I didn't want to use this on you, Lyds. I really, really didn't. But you've left me with no other choice. What else am I supposed to do when you go and bite me? You can't even claim it was an accident. You drew blood."

She stared at him, her nostrils flaring. It took every ounce of self-control not to say anything. She would have to work to gain his trust again.

"Do you have anything to say for yourself?"

Lydia shook her head.

"Surely, you have something. You don't bite someone for no reason."

She stuffed every ounce of her dignity aside. "I'm sorry, Dean. I wasn't thinking. Really, I was just scared. It won't happen again."

He pressed the knife against her throat. "Damn straight it won't."

Lydia swallowed, tears threatening. "I promise. Please, give me another chance."

"You'd like that, wouldn't you? All you've done is prove to me that I can't trust you."

"I'm sorry." A tear ran down her face. "Please."

He pressed the knife into her flesh. Lydia could feel a small amount of blood run down her neck.

"I do like it when you beg." He looked at her with expectation.

Lydia shook. "Dean, think about all the good times we've had. We can have many more."

"That's not begging." He shoved the knife in deeper.

"Please stop. Please." More tears ran down her face.

"Tell me you'll do anything."

"I will."

"Say it!"

"I'll do anything."

Dean sat back, taking the knife with him. "That's what I love to hear. But the problem is I don't know if I can believe you."

Ride

CARA SHOOK IN the seat. She couldn't focus on a thing Corey said. Whatever it was didn't sound important. Cara was sure he was only trying to calm her down, and she couldn't imagine that happening anytime soon.

They drove into their neighborhood, and Corey took the long way, driving by the Harris house. Cara looked over, and noticed a blind halfway up.

"Wait."

Corey stopped the car. "What? Do you see Dean?"

"No, but look."

"What?" he asked.

Men. Cara could never believe how dense they were. "Look up at the window over there." She pointed toward the blind.

"You think that means something?" Corey asked.

"Well, yeah. Lydia's such a perfectionist, she'd never let a blind sit like that."

"What do you think it means? Could she be in there?"

"Maybe."

He swore, and then pulled out his phone. Cara could hear it ringing, and then she heard Bri's voice.

Corey cut her off. "Do you think Lydia could be in her house with Dean? ... I know what you told me." He went on to explain the blind. Cara heard Bri yelling through the phone. She also knew Lydia wouldn't leave the blinds like that, not unless something was wrong.

Corey put the phone away, and then turned to Cara. "I'm going to look around the house. You stay here, and lock the doors until I get back."

"Shouldn't someone call the cops?"

"Bri's on it. Just stay here." Corey got out of the car and then motioned for Cara to lock it.

She pushed the button, locking the doors. Cara watched as Corey hurried to the house, looking inside windows. He walked around until she couldn't see him anymore.

Cara's pulse picked up. The last thing she needed was to run into Dean in her condition.

She clutched the armrest, digging her fingers into it. Sweat broke out on her forehead. The baby moved erratically in her stomach. She rubbed her belly, realizing how important it was that she calm down. She took deep breaths, and focused on the baby. Dean wasn't after her. She was safe in the car.

Finally, her heartbeat returned to normal, and she looked back toward the house. Corey should be back by now. It shouldn't have taken him that long to walk around the house, even if he'd had to climb over the fence. She couldn't recall if there were locks on their gates or not.

"Calm down," she ordered herself. Maybe Corey had just found a way in. She looked back up toward the window. The blind was still messed up.

Her phone rang, startling her. It was Bri. Probably wanting to know where Corey was.

"Hi, Bri."

"What's going on? Why isn't Corey answering his phone?"

"He's looking around the house."

"Is he okay?"

"I'm sure he is. He's smart."

"Yeah, but if Dean has a gun, that doesn't matter." Bri's voice cracked.

"Corey's smart. He's not going to walk into a situation and do something stupid. He knows you and the girls are his first priority."

"Right. You're exactly right."

They were quiet for a minute. Cara watched the house, waiting for Corey to show.

"Do you see him yet?"

"No. I'm sure he's fine."

Sirens sounded in the distance.

"You called the police, right?" Cara asked.

"Yeah, they should be on the way over there now."

"I think I hear them."

"Oh, thank God." Bri let out a long breath. "Do you see them?"

Cara turned the rear view mirror so she could see behind her. "I see the lights flashing."

Ambush

L YDIA'S HEART NEARLY exploded out of her chest, staring at Dean as he
played with the knife that now had a little of her blood on it. "You
can trust me, Dean. I swear."

"After the stunt you just pulled?" He stuck the sharp end of the knife
underneath his nail, flicking out dirt. "That's from you making me chase
you in those woods."

Her mind raced. She had to prove trustworthy before she became his
next victim. "Think of everything I've done for you, sweetie. Decorated
this room just the way you like. Remember? You didn't want to go
shopping, so I did all, getting your opinion every step of the way."

"You just bit me, Lydia." He set the knife aside.

"I can't help it. You tied me up."

"So you can't control yourself?" He asked, digging dirt out of another
nail. "That doesn't instill confidence in me."

"No, I mean… don't get me wrong. I have full self-control, I just…."
How would she talk her way out of it and keep his trust? She took a deep
breath. "Dean, I love you. I regret biting you. It was wrong of me to do
that. How could I risk injuring those perfect arms? You know how I've
always loved your muscles."

He looked up, raising an eyebrow.

"I wish I could feel them right now, baby."

"You do?" He set the knife down.

Lydia forced her most sultry expression. "Let me run my hands up
and down them, Dean. Feel how strong and powerful you are."

He sat up taller. "Then what? I'd have to loosen the ropes."

"I won't try to hurt you again. I learned my lesson. The only thing I want is to stand at your side. Take me traveling with you, like you said. We haven't acted like a married couple in so long. It'll be like a second honeymoon."

"That does sound nice, but I need to know I can trust you. I'm just not convinced yet." He rubbed the bite.

Lydia scooted closer. "What can I do to prove my loyalty?"

He looked deep in thought. "I'll just have to give you the benefit of the doubt. Just know that I won't hesitate to cut you again—only worse next time."

Lydia jumped, her pulse racing.

"I've loved you since the moment I laid eyes you, Lydia. You're really the only one for me—but I won't hesitate to add you to my list. Do you understand?"

She swallowed. "Yes."

"I don't want to hurt you, but if you make me, I will." He narrowed his eyes. "Have I made myself clear?"

"Crystal."

"Let me see those ropes."

Lydia turned her back to him. She heard him slicing through the knots.

"Oops," he said, and then Lydia felt a cut on her wrist.

She gasped.

"Don't worry, it's not too deep. Just like your neck. Think of it as a reminder to behave."

Lydia nodded her head. At least she would be free of the ropes. Once she had the freedom to move around, she could figure out how to get out of the house, and as far away from Dean as possible.

One thing at a time.

"Ouch!" she cried as he nicked her on the other wrist.

"So sorry." The corners of his mouth twitched.

She took a deep breath. "I know you didn't mean it, dear."

"Oh, I meant it. Just need to make sure to keep you in line. You asked how you can show me your loyalty—trust me enough to let you hurt you."

Lydia felt blood drain from her face. Exactly how far did he intend to go? She cleared her throat. "Of course, Dean. That's the least I could do to prove my love to you."

"That's my girl." He pulled the ropes away from her arms.

Lydia brought her arms back in front of her. She cried out in pain. Her arms were sore from having been behind her for so long.

"Are you okay, Lyds?" Dean asked. He rubbed her shoulders. "Does that help?"

She nodded, tears stinging her eyes. She blinked them away before Dean could see them.

"Now for those ropes around your ankles." He looked at her, his eyes lighting up as though excited.

Lydia's breath caught. Was he going to cut her ankles, too? She rubbed the cuts on her wrists, getting blood on her fingers.

He reached down and pulled her feet up onto the bed, making it hard for her to balance. She had to put her hands on the bedspread to keep from falling over. Blood got on the white fabric, and she quickly covered it with her hand before Dean could see it.

"Look at your poor feet," he said, rubbing her soles. "You shouldn't have run away from me like that barefoot."

Lydia grimaced, trying not to react from the pain.

He rubbed harder. "Does that hurt?"

"It's…a little…sore." She gritted her teeth.

"Oh, that's too bad," Dean said, his tone mocking. He pushed harder on her feet. "Well, let's get this rope off you, and then we can get you cleaned up."

She nodded, biting her tongue. The pain spread from her feet up into her legs.

"You don't mind me hurting you, do you?" he asked, holding the knife near the knot.

"Go ahead," she whispered. "Anything to let you know how much you can trust me."

Dean grinned. "You don't know how happy this makes me." He cut the rope in short, swift motions.

Lydia couldn't help watching. She knew he was going to cut her, but she didn't know when. It was like one of the jack-in-the-box toys that had always scared her as a child, always jumping up when she least expected it.

He continued to cut at the rope, but not her. She relaxed. Maybe he finally trusted her enough to stop cutting into her skin.

"How are you doing, Lyds?" He rubbed her knee.

She forced a smile. "Just glad to be back on good terms with you again, sweetie."

"You just keep making me happier and happier."

Lydia let out a sigh of relief. She continued watching him. He was almost all the way through the rope.

Slice.

His hand moved from the rope to her ankle, cutting her skin about two inches.

She bit her tongue and arched her back, trying to keep from crying out in pain.

"Oh, are you okay?" he asked.

Lydia looked at him and nodded, her face contorted with pain.

"Well, I'm almost done. Then we can discuss our plans."

She nodded her head. Finally finding her voice, she said, "Can't wait."

"You sure you're okay?" he asked. "Your voice sounds strained."

"Couldn't be better."

"Good." He cut into the rope one more time and it came loose.

Lydia pulled her knees up to her chest and rubbed the rope burns.

A thud sounded downstairs.

Dean's eyes widened. "What was that?"

Lydia backed away. "I don't know."

Something sounded from downstairs, sounding like a dull thud.

He stuck the knife in his pocket and grabbed Lydia's arm, squeezing tight. His nails dug into her flesh. "Come on."

Lydia's heart pounded all the harder, even though she hadn't thought it could go any faster. Dean dragged her down the stairs, making it difficult for her to keep up without stumbling. The normally-soft carpeting felt like razor blades on her sore, torn-up feet.

Another noise sounded from downstairs, but this time it was softer.

"Is someone down here?" Dean called as he stepped down from the last step. He yanked Lydia down, making her stumble. She landed against him, and he turned, giving her a dirty look. He turned back toward the rest of the downstairs. "I said—is anyone here?"

Nothing.

Lydia's breathing quickened, making it hard to focus. Someone had to be there. They'd heard the noises, and they didn't have any animals. Did someone see the blinds and try to sneak in?

Dean walked toward the front door, pulling on Lydia's arms. She grimaced. His nails continued digging into her skin, one dug into a cut, making it hurt all the more.

Nothing looked out of place there. Dean put his finger over his mouth and dragged Lydia around to the other side of the stairs. He swore and then yanked her into his office.

The window sat open and several things from his desk were scattered around on the floor, broken.

Dean shoved Lydia against the wall and then held up the knife, obviously as a warning not to try anything. He pulled a key out from another pocket and unlocked one of the drawers in his desk. He pulled out a gun and stuffed it into his pants at the waist.

He let go, letting his shirt cover the gun. Then he grabbed Lydia and walked out of the office with her in front of him—his human shield.

"Who's down here?" Dean called.

Lydia knew whoever it was wouldn't answer, and she prayed that it was someone there to help her. She wasn't the praying type, but if she ever needed it, now was the time.

Something caught her eye in the living room.

It was Corey. He stood pressed against the wall.

Lydia's eyes widened and her mouth gaped open.

Corey put his finger to his mouth. He had a baseball bat in the other hand.

She pointed in the direction of the other room. "I think I see something in there."

"Where?" asked Dean.

"Over there. It looks like someone trying to hide."

He squeezed her arm tighter, pulling her along.

She let a silent sigh of relief, glad that Dean hadn't seen Corey. Now that Dean had a gun on him, Corey didn't stand a chance against him.

"I don't see anything." Dean turned around, pulling Lydia with him.

Corey stood in the hallway only about a foot from them. He held the bat up.

"What are you doing here, Corey?" Dean demanded.

"My wife was afraid Lydia was in trouble. I get the impression she was right."

"You broke into my house based on a stupid woman's fears?"

Anger covered Corey's face and he stepped forward. "My wife isn't stupid, you piece of—"

"All women are stupid, and so are you if you haven't figured that out." Dean pulled Lydia closer to him.

"You are something else," Corey said. "Why don't you let go of Lydia and we can talk about whatever you two are disagreeing about?"

"I have a better idea," Dean said. He pulled out his knife and held it to Lydia's throat.

She gasped, trying not to move. It wouldn't take much for the knife to dig into her skin from the way it pressed against her. Lydia stared at Corey, begging him with her eyes to do something to help.

"Easy," Corey said, putting a hand up. "That's not necessary."

"How about you leave my house? Now." Dean put more pressure on the knife, cutting ever so slightly into Lydia's skin again.

Corey lowered the bat. "Not while you have a knife to Lydia's throat. That's not cool, dude. You drop the knife and I'll drop the bat. Sound like a good deal?"

Dean laughed. "How about you leave us alone, and I don't call the cops?"

"When you're threatening your wife's life? I don't think so. We both know who the cops would side with."

"Just get out of here! This doesn't concern you, Corey. You're always butting in where you don't belong."

Sirens sounded outside, the noise echoing off the hardwood floors from the open window in Dean's office.

Dean let out a string of profanities. "Did you call the cops?" he asked Corey, loosening his grip on Lydia slightly.

"No," Corey said, "I didn't. Bri might have, though. So, you really should consider letting Lydia go, especially with the blood dripping down onto her shirt."

"What?" Dean exclaimed. He let go and turned Lydia around. "There's no blood dripping—"

Lydia pulled away and ran for Corey. She stood behind him and he put the baseball bat out toward Dean. "Don't come near us."

Dean slid his hand down toward his gun, keeping his hand there.

There was a loud knock on the door. "Police!"

Fear covered Dean's face. He was trapped between a laundry room with no outside doors or windows and Corey and Lydia. "Move, Corey. Get out of my way before I have to hurt you."

The police pounded on the door again. "Open up, or we'll be forced to break down the door."

Lydia screamed as loudly as she could.

With that, she heard the sounds of the door being broken down. Footsteps thundered. It sounded like an army. She could hear them scouring the front of the house.

"Over here!" Lydia yelled.

Dean pulled out his gun and aimed it at Corey and her.

Corey turned around and threw himself on top of Lydia, sending them both onto the ground.

A shot rang out, echoing so loud that it hurt Lydia's ears.

"Stay down," Corey told her.

Not that she could go anywhere with his weight on her.

Footsteps approached, and Lydia saw eight feet around her.

"Put the gun down."

"You can't take me," Dean said.

Another shot sounded, but Lydia couldn't tell if it came from the officers or Dean. No one fell to the ground, much to her relief. But before she could look around, yet another one rang out and Dean fell to the ground, swearing.

Lydia cried out in surprise and fear. She looked over at him to see that he clutched his leg and blood pooled on the floor. He picked the gun up from where it fell and he aimed it at the officers, cussing them out.

"Put the gun down or we shoot you in the heart next time."

"You won't take me that easily. I'm already down—you won't shoot."

"Shut up," Lydia whispered.

Dean turned the weapon to Lydia. "I'll shoot her!"

"Drop the weapon." An officer stepped forward. He aimed his gun at Dean's head.

"No."

A gunshot sounded.

It took Lydia a moment to realize it came from the cops.

The bullet barely missed Dean.

He dropped his gun to the floor.

It was over.

Boxed

LYDIA SHOVED THE last box into the moving truck. Tom stepped beside her and closed the door, locking it. Lydia turned to her friends. "Thanks so much for helping."

"Are you sure you won't come to the hospital with us?" Savannah asked.

Lydia shook her head. "I can't look at Cara, and especially not the baby."

Bri bumped Lydia playfully. "I hear she looks like an Ewok."

"Be nice," Corey said, winking at Bri. He turned to Lydia. "Cara feels really bad about everything that happened."

"Yeah," Bri said, "but Lydia has every right to hate her."

"I don't hate her," Lydia said, feeling defensive. "I just can't look at her or Dean's... the baby."

"Nobody could blame you for that," Savannah said.

Tom checked the back door of the truck, and then turned to Lydia. "Are you sure you don't want Corey and me to follow you? You're going to need help unpacking."

Lydia's cheeks warmed. "I do have help, but thanks."

Bri raised an eyebrow. "Why do you look embarrassed, sweetie?"

"I just have help, that's all."

"Is it Toby?" Savannah asked.

"Wait," Bri said. "Is he the new mystery guy?"

Lydia looked away. "Maybe. I didn't want to say anything until I knew it was serious."

Savannah took her hand. "He's helping you unpack. I'd say it sounds fairly serious."

"Okay, okay," Lydia admitted. "We've been seeing a lot of each other. He doesn't mind our age difference or the fact that my ex is in prison for life for nearly a dozen murders."

"At least you're not the one in prison," Corey joked.

"Oh, babe." Bri gave him a shove. "Stop."

"Who would've thought he was using his job as cover for murdering people?" Savannah asked, shaking her head. "And we all thought it was just affairs."

"So, he killed more than you first thought?" Tom asked Lydia, leaning against the truck. He pulled Savannah close and wrapped his arms around her.

"Twice as many," Lydia said.

"At least you get to keep all the stuff," Savannah said.

Bri grinned. "And our Lydia is going to get a true happily ever after."

Savannah pulled away from Tom and hugged Lydia. "I'm so happy for you. Wanna join us for drinks later? We can take you out for dinner. Bring Toby. It would be great for all six of us to hang out."

"Can we make it a rain check?" Lydia asked. "That sounds wonderful, but after we get some of my stuff unpacked, Toby's going to take me to his ranch to ride horses. Then we're going to get his prize horse, Flash, ready for another show."

"Aww," Bri gushed. "I'm so happy for you."

"Me, too," Savannah said. "You better not forget about us."

"How could I?" Lydia asked. "Group hug."

They all hugged, and then Bri dragged Lydia to the front of the truck. "Better not leave that cute cowboy waiting."

If you enjoyed Dean's List, you'll like Gone—the story that inspired Dean's List.

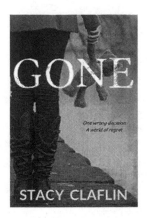

About

Macy Mercer only wants a little independence. Eager to prove herself grown up, she goes to a dark, secluded park. She's supposed to meet the boy of her dreams who she met online. But the cute fifteen year old was a fantasy, his pictures fake. She finds herself face to face with Chester Woodran, a man capable of murder.

Distraught over his own missing daughter, Chester insists that Macy replace his lost girl. He locks Macy up, withholds food, and roughs her up, demanding that she call him dad. Under duress from his constant threats and mind games, her hold on reality starts to slip. Clinging to her memories is the only way of holding onto her true identity, not believing that she is Chester's daughter. Otherwise she may never see her family again.

Preview of Gone

SITTING IN HIS warm truck across from the park, Chester Woodran watched her walk across the open field. An overhead light turned on as she passed under it in the dusk. Her long, dark hair swished back and forth behind her. She wandered around the playground, walking between the climbers and slides until she stopped in front of the swings.

He had spent hours watching her. Studying her. He knew her almost better than she knew herself.

The moment of truth would arrive soon. She'd come a few minutes early, but he wouldn't deviate from the schedule. He would act exactly on time. He'd laid the groundwork. He wasn't going to let her change a thing.

Chester pulled out his phone and scrolled through the pictures, stopping at his favorite. It was the girl in the park for sure, although he couldn't see the details of her face up close yet. He would have to wait a few minutes.

From the phone, her light brown eyes shone at him. Her shy, almost insecure face smiled sweetly.

His heart sped up at the thought of many weeks of work coming together at long last. The waiting was about to end.

Clenching the steering wheel with all his might, he took several deep breaths to calm himself. Every precaution had been taken. Prepared with painstaking care. There was no chance of anything going wrong so long as he stayed with the plan.

The alarm on his digital wristwatch beeped. He turned it off and then leaned back into the seat, adjusting his over-sized glasses.

It was time.

More Information.

stacyclaflin.com/books/gone/

Already read Gone?

Rusty and Luke will have their own thrilling stories coming soon!

Other books by Stacy Claflin

Gone series
Gone
Held
Over
Complete Trilogy
Dean's List

The Transformed Series
Deception (#1)
Betrayal (#2)
Forgotten (#3)
Silent Bite (#3.5)
Ascension (#4)
Duplicity (#5)
Sacrifice (#6)
Destroyed (#7)
Hidden Intentions (novel)
A Long Time Coming (Short Story)
Fallen (Novella)
Taken (Novella)

Coming Soon
#8

Seaside Hunters (Sweet Romance)
Seaside Surprises (Now Available)
Seaside Heartbeats (Coming Soon)
Seaside Dances (Coming Soon)
Seaside Kisses (Coming Soon)
Seaside Christmas (Coming Soon)

Other books
Chasing Mercy
Searching for Mercy

Visit StacyClaflin.com for details.

Sign up for new release updates.
stacyclaflin.com/newsletter

Want to hang out and talk about books? Join My Book Hangout and participate in the discussions. There are also exclusive giveaways, sneak peeks and more. Sometimes the members offer opinions on book covers too. You never know what you'll find.
facebook.com/groups/stacyclaflinbooks

Author's Note

Thanks so much for reading Dean's List. This was a fun book to write since I was able to revisit some of the characters from Gone. Lydia is one that grew on me the more that I wrote her in Gone as she grew to show her deeper sides. I really enjoyed getting to know her better through this story.

That's one of the reasons I really like writing side stories in a series. And if you like them as much as I do, you'll be excited to know that there are stories planned for both Rusty and Luke.

Do you have a favorite character that you would like to see get a book of his or her own? Let me know! Contact me (stacyclaflin.com/contact) and tell me who you'd like to see. That's why Luke is on my list of stories to write—readers asked for it.

If you enjoyed this book, please consider leaving a review wherever you purchased it. Not only will your review help me to better understand what you like—so I can give you more of it!—but it will also help other readers find my work. Reviews can be short—just share your honest thoughts. That's it.

Want to know when I have a new release? Sign up here (stacyclaflin.com/newsletter) for new release updates. You'll even get a free book!

I've spent many hours writing, re-writing, and editing this work. I even put together a team who helped with the editing process. As it is impossible to find every single error, if you find any, please contact me through my website and let me know. Then I can fix them for future editions.

Thank you for your support!
~Stacy

Made in the USA
San Bernardino, CA
15 January 2020